GYPSY GOLD

/ / / /

H.P MALLORY
&
J.R. RAIN

THE HAVEN HOLLOW SERIES

Poppy's Potions

Published by
Rain Press

Printed in the United States of America.

ISBN- 9798864675755

Chapter One

The drops of sandalwood extract gave the potion a warm amber color as it simmered gently on the little hot plate I kept at the shop.

It was now October which meant the days had started getting shorter again, the street lamps lining Main Street already coming on, and I hadn't had a customer for almost an hour.

There was always a little lull in business after the summer tourist season, and before the holiday shopping took off, so this wasn't exactly unusual. And once we were a couple of weeks out from Halloween, then everything would pick up again. The little hiatus gave me a chance to restock and prepare for the next rush. Looking around my shop, Poppy's Potions, and seeing shelves full of an array of little glass bottles and anointed beeswax candles was pretty satisfying. And, of course, not to forget all the dreamcatchers—those were always a popular item.

Warm contentment settled in my chest, glowing like a candle flame, when I heard my son laugh in the shop's little back room. Finn was in the middle of getting a magic lesson from Andre. While the idea of my son having the kind of magic that could put him in dangerous situations as he attempted to help people still scared the heck out of me, it was better for him to get training than to just go it alone and hope for the best.

And, I trusted Andre to look out for Finn, to do right by him. Not just because Andre was my soulmate (and I don't mean that in a cliche, sappy sort of way—he literally was my soulmate, if the red ribbons that bound us had anything to say about it). But because Andre was a good man who cared about Finn.

Soulmate.

The word and, of course, the meaning still felt new and strange to me, but in a good way. I couldn't stop the smile from curling my lips—couldn't stop it even if I'd tried. It just—well, this was new to me and it was exciting—exhilarating really. I'd always felt a connection with

Andre—an intensity I'd never understood. And I'd felt it from the instant we'd met. That connection had felt a lot like I'd known him all my life, like I'd just been waiting for him to come walking around the next corner.

I had a soulmate.

As soon as the thought crossed my mind again (okay, for the twentieth time today), that little bit of melancholy sank back in. Because, yes I had a soulmate, but one who was leaving.

Oh, not forever.

Not even for very long, really.

But this whole relationship between us was still so new for me. Finding out that we were fated for one another, but also understanding just what that meant—well, that took some time. Initially, Andre and I had agreed to take things slowly—just to start as friends and basically see where we ended up. A few weeks ago we'd finally agreed to take things to the next level, to start... dating. And, well, it was a big step. For both of us. So, any separation felt like it was too long. Sometimes just saying goodnight to Andre felt like it was too much distance, which was ridiculous, because he lived up the street from me.

As to this new relationship between us—as I mentioned, it was really, very new. In that, we (or I) had been beating around the bush, not wanting to commit to anything, because I was so afraid of messing it up. But once Andre assured me that we could take things slowly, that we wouldn't rush the romance part, I agreed, and here we were. And we were taking things *really* slowly. Almost painfully slowly. The most we'd done, in the physical department, was kiss.

I gave myself a little shake. I was in my forties, and a single mom, I didn't need to go mooning over a man like I was a silly teenager again. No matter how brilliant, and kind, and handsome that man was. And no matter how his British accent made shivers run up and down my spine. And–

The potion on the burner had started bubbling, its color darkening, and I jerked my thoughts back to the task at hand. Walking over, I gave it a little stir, soothing it back down to a slow simmer once more.

It was just three weeks that Andre and I had been dating. That was nothing—no time at all. Andre had moved all the way to Haven Hollow from Portland months before—because he felt it his calling to train Finn in the art of being a magician. He'd bought the farmhouse up the road, and completely resettled his life just to mentor Finn. But that didn't mean Andre didn't still have his own work—of course, he still did. So that meant back on the road for him since he was traveling to do a series of performances, stage magic, not the supernatural kind. He was leaving today and then he'd be home again.

And I couldn't wait until he was home again.

It was the first time Andre was leaving since he'd told me about the bond between us, so maybe that was the reason why his trip was hitting me so hard. It felt like we had so many years to catch up on—so many unanswered questions regarding this strange and incredible bond between us. I still didn't really understand what it meant—how it could be or why. All I knew was that it just was.

Something strange uncoiled in my chest then, and the potion gave a little warning burble. I took a couple deep breaths and tried to get my emotions back under control, forcing my attention to hone in on the potion and away from my heart.

Potions were my thing. They were the shape my magic took, just like my mother and grandmother before me. I came from a long line of what are called 'Gypsy Travellers', and the women of my lineage had always been strong in potion magic. Finn was kind of an outlier. Magic tended to prefer women, but the men in my family still managed to have small quirks and gifts—for example, one of my uncles could sniff out mushrooms. Finn's magic (other than being a magician) was that he could tell when someone was lying, which was a pretty strong gift. And, that had been before we'd found out that he had the ability to become a Magician.

Speaking of family, I'd actually recently been introduced to a cousin of mine I'd never even known I'd had—Lydia Morton had moved to Haven Hollow in order to seek the safety of a Hollow. I didn't understand much about what was going on with her (and thought it too rude to ask), but from what she'd explained to me when Finn and I had had her over for dinner was that she was basically possessed by a witch. She was a gypsy like me, but had never been much good with magic. Now, she was trying to figure exactly what she was, and she was trying to make sense of this new life she was now leading. I hadn't seen much of my new cousin because, strangely enough, Angelo Stendham had pretty much appointed himself as her personal bodyguard and he kept her under strict watch 24-7. Apparently, he was worried some big bad was out to get her. All I knew was that I didn't want Finn to get involved with one more dangerous situation, so I'd kept my distance just as much as Lydia was keeping hers.

But things had been changing for me, too—

really ever since I'd moved to Haven Hollow, a town where the supernatural hunkered down to play nice with their mundane neighbors. Hollows were supposed to be safe places for everyone, but there had been a lot of turmoil in our little town lately. Factions were forming, and people were targeting our Hollow specifically. Things were getting more and more dangerous. And Lydia moving here was just another example of how.

That was why, when my witch BFF, Wanda, had offered me a spot in her newly formed coven, even though I wasn't a witch, I'd taken her up on her offer. Being a founding member of the coven gave me some protection, and that protection extended to Finn, too. Everyone who was anyone would know that if they came after me or my son, there would be a lot of really angry witches on their doorstep. And that was something no one wanted. Furthermore, considering the coven also had a few wild cards in it, a Blood Witch and Blood Warlock to name a couple, most sensible people would give Finn and me a very wide berth.

The whole reason why witches even formed covens was to mingle their magic across the bonds of the members. That mingling of magic made each witch stronger, more magically powerful. But I wasn't a witch, and I didn't have that sort of magic. So, I'd thought joining the coven would be in name only—a token offer from a very close friend who was trying to keep me and my son safe.

It hadn't exactly turned out that way, though.

I'd felt it when the bonds formed between all the members of Scapegrace Coven, and ever since, my magic had been changing, becoming something other than the talent I'd had ever since I was a little girl. This new power within me was strange, and honestly a little bit frightening. I did my best to keep it under control, to keep it from seeping out, but eventually, I was really going to have to talk to Wanda about it.

If I could just figure out how to bring it up without sounding like an ingrate. Not to mention that Wanda was dealing with her own issues at the moment—vampire issues.

With the potion returned to its mellow golden color, I gave it a careful stir and picked up the last ingredient. I hadn't made this particular potion for years, but I was excited to revisit it. The potion was mostly a party trick, a joke between friends, or something flashy meant to impress. I'd never thought it would sell in the shop, so I'd never bothered with it. But then I'd been flipping through my family potion book, and I'd come across it again. It was fairly simple, and fun, and I'd thought it might make a cute little going away present for Andre, something to wow the kids with at his performance.

I dropped in the three flakes of Pyrite into the beaker, and even though Fool's Gold didn't dissolve, the flakes melted into the potion, filling the liquid with soft sparkles, like I'd mixed in gold glitter.

It brought back a lot of memories. *Gypsy Gold* was one of the first potions my grandmother had taught me to brew, since it was easy and flashy and the results were pretty obvious. It made for an interesting beginner potion and, consequently, it was one of the first I'd ever learned.

Once the potion had cooled, and the night outside got even chillier, the shadows spinning out from between the buildings, I carefully decanted the glittering potion into a glass vial. This particular vial was a pretty pale yellow and the shimmering gold sparkles of the potion shined right through.

That was when Andre and Finn emerged from the back room, Finn talking animatedly, gesturing with his arms. His sleeves were rolled up, so I caught the flash of stark black numbers on his skin, the marks left when a Magician mastered a new trick, like a magical tattoo. There were more black numbers on his arms now than the last time I'd checked, to the point that they were starting to look a little crowded.

I took a deep breath and looked away, careful to keep my smile in place. I was still worried about Finn learning this sort of magic. The more power he got, the more likely it was that he'd start getting pulled into all the troubles going on in the Hollow, and I just couldn't allow that (hence why I didn't want him to know much about whatever was going on with Lydia). Finn was fourteen, barely even a teenager, and my only son, my only child. So, it was probably no wonder I was so protective of him. Regardless, I was doing everything in my power to ensure he never put himself in another compromising position. And if that meant I had to keep my distance from my new family member, well then it was what I'd have to do.

Even though I was nervous about Finn's magic, I did my best to hide my worry. To be fair, even if I forbid Finn from learning, and Andre from teaching him, Finn could just dream walk in his sleep, and, in doing so, he'd learn magic from Ouire, his grimoire, but he'd do it while sleeping. The magical book had taught him in the past, before Andre ever returned to the Hollow, and it was sort of like Finn's pet, in a way. At least, the thing was animated and acted like a happy dog, always wagging this way and that. Regardless, I didn't want Finn dream walking in order to learn his art. And I didn't have any way to control what the book decided to teach him, so I figured it was best to allow him to learn from Andre and do my best to keep him safe. And, again, I trusted Andre with all my heart.

Chapter Two

I dusted my hands off, setting the potion bottle to one side. "Hey, guys. All finished?"

"Yeah, Mom." Finn smiled, but it wasn't his usual big sunny grin. I knew he wasn't looking forward to Andre leaving town, either, even if it was just for a few weeks. Since Andre had moved to Haven Hollow, the two of them had become very close.

"Finn, can you lock the door and flip the sign to closed, please?" I double checked that the hotplate was turned off and then unplugged it. I was still a bit paranoid about things in my life going wrong, but it seemed that the aura of bad luck I'd been put under over the summer was well and truly gone. I hadn't had so much as a stubbed toe in the last couple of months.

And thank God for that.

"Sure," Finn called back as he bounced over to the door. He was always either full of energy after a lesson, or absolutely drained, with no in between. At least he hadn't had a fainting spell recently. Those had been really scary. Beyond scary actually. Andre still couldn't say what had caused such an extreme response in the first place, but luckily, Finn had been doing a better job of conserving his energy.

Ouire bounded past me, chasing after Finn, running on the corners of his cover, more like a dog than a book. Even the red ribbon bookmark flapped behind him, like a wagging tail. The second Finn stepped away from the door, Ouire leapt into his arms like an over eager pet. It was sweet. I knew they were going to miss each other, but at least Finn and Ouire could visit in dreams.

"How's he doing?" I asked quietly when Andre reached the counter, a smile on his incredibly handsome face.

Sometimes I still struggled to believe that such an amazing man was fated to me. Tall and built like a swimmer, Andre tended towards dark sweaters and slacks, even when he was going for casual. This particular charcoal gray sweater made his shoulders appear even wider. His eyes were a perfect pale blue, with just a few lines at their corners, while his dark hair had just started to thread with gray. I had to curl my hands into loose fists to keep from reaching for him. I always wanted to touch him—the feeling was almost like a driving force and sometimes I had to forcibly keep my fingers clasped behind my back. Now was no different—the desire to trace my fingers over the sharp angle of his jaw, his cheekbones, the straight line of his nose—well, it was almost suffocating.

He must have felt at least a little bit of the same pull, because he brushed the tips of his fingers over the back of my hand, his touch as soft as a butterfly's wings. I watched with a little smile as he took a deep breath and pulled his hand back, clasping both behind his back, mimicking me. Truly, this soulmate business could sometimes be a bit tedious when you were constantly fighting the need to touch one another. While I might have wanted to give into the need, I also didn't want to make Finn uncomfortable with too many public displays of affection. I was and always would be a mother first.

"He's doing brilliantly, really." Andre tipped his face towards the door to where Finn and Ouire were having a cuddle, which then turned into a wrestle as the book tickled my son and he belched out a laugh in response. "Finn really is a natural. He's going to be an incredible Magician one day."

Warmth kindled in my chest. I'd always known Finn was special, but it was nice to have other people recognize it, as well. And not just 'other people' but this particular person.

Laughing, Finn spun around with the book in his arms. "Oh, Andre, did you want to see my science fair project?"

"Of course, I do." Andre grinned and shot me a wink before he moved towards the table where Finn had set up his experiment.

He'd insisted on doing the entire thing on his own, from research to getting the materials, and setting the experiment up. I'd tried to take that as an example of his burgeoning independence and not just him wanting his mom to butt out. Regardless, I was proud of the work he'd put into the experiment, and I knew Finn was proud of it too.

He set Ouire down so that he could show off the two plastic bottles that he'd carefully assembled together, walking Andre through the steps, and showing him how the whole thing worked.

"And then that creates a whirlpool," Finn crowed happily as the water in the bottles spun itself into a water spout like a captive hurricane. "Isn't it cool?"

"Very cool," Andre said with real enthusiasm as he crouched down to get a better look at the process.

I watched them quietly, a small smile on my lips. It made me so very happy to know that my son loved Andre as much as I did—that Andre, a man who had never had children of his own, was such a natural with my son. Furthermore, Andre never overstepped his boundaries—he was first and foremost a friend to Finn and then he was a teacher. But he never played the part of parent and I appreciated that. I was sure Finn did too.

Finn raked his pale hair back off his forehead with one hand, still beaming. "You should see my friend Sophie's experiment. It's so cool. She's doing this whole presentation on plant hybridization, where she managed to graft part of an orange branch onto an apple tree. She's waiting to see if the tree will grow apples and oranges." Finn shook his head, amazed. "She's so smart."

She was. I'd met her a couple times, when Finn dragged some kids home for homework sessions. From what I could gather, Sophie was a quiet girl with glasses, kind and laughed at every one of Finn's jokes (which was, no doubt, part of the reason he liked to have her around). She was also very clever and fully human. Sometimes, with all the curses, and the faerie civil wars, and the rampaging demons, it was easy to lose track of just how much normal humans were capable of. And it was nice.

"Mr. Lannister, he's our science teacher—well, he doesn't like it."

"He doesn't like what?" Andre asked Finn who was now frowning.

Finn's face darkened. "He doesn't like Sophie's experiment. He keeps telling her that her experiment is flawed and won't work, even though she has lots of papers that prove you can graft an orange tree branch to an apple tree. She's been working on it really hard. I think partly just to prove him wrong."

"I'm sure she will prove him wrong," Andre assured him. "She sounds brilliant."

"Speaking of experiments," I said, beckoning them both back over to the counter. "I made a little something fun for you, Andre."

Finn bent down to look at the little yellow bottle from a couple different angles, his brows wrinkling together. "It's sparkly. I've never seen a sparkly one before."

I made a little hum and waggled my eyebrows as I tugged the stopper out of the bottle. "And now, for your viewing pleasure," I started, putting on a deep voice as I attempted to sound like the quintessential salesman, "I present to you... *Gypsy Gold*!"

Andre looked at me with a laugh and there was true warmth in his eyes. I wasn't the stage magician that Andre was, certainly, but I tried to put on a little flourish as I tugged the closest thing on the counter, the stapler in this case, closer to me.

Finn giggled, and Andre smiled, so I thought I'd done pretty well.

Slowly, carefully, I dripped the potion onto the stapler, and the sparkling liquid flowed over the red plastic, instantly turning the stapler into glittering gold.

"Whoa, cool!" Finn leaned forward until his nose almost touched it. Even Andre looked surprised.

I had to admit, the potion worked perfectly. The gold color had spread across both plastic and metal, until it looked like the whole stapler was now shimmering gold. The spell couldn't make real gold, of course, and there was a particular shine to it that made it clear that it was Fool's Gold and not twenty-four carats, but it was fun and showy, and it usually made people laugh.

"*Gypsy Gold*, eh?" Andre asked.

I nodded as I flicked my fingers towards the stapler. "It only works for an hour or so before the magic fades and the object goes back to whatever it was. I thought you might like to take a vial of it with you for your shows. I figured the kids might like it."

The smile that stretched across Andre's face was slow and sweet as he examined the stapler, watching the light reflect off its shiny surface. "They absolutely will. This is incredible, Poppy." Then he looked up at me once more and as soon as our eyes connected, I swallowed hard. "Really, you're amazing."

"Right?" Finn wrapped his arms around me. "She's the coolest."

A flush burned up into my face, turning my cheeks bright red. Maybe it was silly, but having my teenage son think I was cool was kind of great. And Andre's appreciative eyes weren't so bad, either. In fact, they were making a hot blush creep up my neck and I suddenly felt much hotter than I had a second ago.

I slid the bottle towards Andre, and he picked it up with gentle hands. I loved his hands, strong with long fingers, and he moved them so deliberately. 'Deft', that was the word. Then I realized I was staring and the blush that had started up my neck suddenly came roaring across my cheeks.

I wanted to smack myself. I felt like a teenager again with her first crush. Everything Andre did was somehow both familiar, and thrilling, and I was so worried about making a fool of myself.

I cleared my throat. "Just make sure you don't spill it, because that wouldn't be good."

Andre laughed, the sound low and rumbling and delicious. "Gold trousers might be a bit hard to explain."

Finn folded his arms on the counter, and leaned forward, his mouth turned down at the corners just a little, like he was fighting not to sulk. "How long are you going for, again?" he asked as he looked at Andre.

"Just three weeks." Andre reached out to ruffle Finn's hair. "I'll be back before you know it, good lad."

Recently, Andre had started referring to Finn as 'good lad' or 'my boy' and Finn seemed to grin even more broadly every time he did. It was moments like these when I remembered that Finn hadn't ever had the benefit of growing up with a dad. His biological father had quit the scene as soon as I'd found out I was pregnant and so I'd raised Finn alone. Coming to Haven Hollow had been wonderful for us both because suddenly Finn had many able and kind male figures in his life to look up to—Roy the sasquatch, Lorcan the vampire, and Marty—a man who had been my best friend, until recently.

Thoughts of Marty always left a sadness

within me, so I tried not to focus on them or him too much. Instead, I brought my attention back to my son, who was looking up at... at *my boyfriend* with the biggest grin.

But then Finn heaved a huge sigh, the kind that only teenagers seem able to manage. And I understood exactly how he was feeling, because I was looking forward to Andre leaving about as much as Finn was.

Though I did feel warm satisfaction curling through me when Andre slipped the potion I'd made for him into his pocket.

"Come on, it's late." I reached under the counter to grab my purse from where I'd stashed it. "Why don't we head up the street to the Half-Moon and grab some dinner before we drive home?"

"And dessert?" Finn glanced up, his eyes shining.

It was funny, sometimes. I could look into my son's face and see the man I knew he was going to grow up to become. And other times, I could see the little boy he used to be, freckle-cheeked with a gapped tooth smile and a shock of white-blonde hair that stuck in every direction. And it was the little boy I saw right now—especially when he got this excited about the prospect of pie.

"Of course," I told him as we headed for the

door. Andre slipped one arm around my shoulders and the other arm around Finn's and we both leaned into him, as if the three of us had always been a family.

Maybe something sweet would ease the bitterness of having to say goodbye, even if it was just for a few weeks.

Chapter Three

Luckily enough, the next few weeks were so busy that the time seemed to fly by.

We had a sudden rush of tourists in town (mid to late October was one of the busiest times in Haven Hollow, along with Christmas) and the orders were flowing in. While we didn't have the same kind of foliage tourism that the east coast got, Haven Hollow had its own fall weather frequenters who would ooh and aah at the showy orange and red of the changing trees. Closer to Halloween (maybe the week before), we'd see an even bigger burst of crowds, drawn in by Sweeter Haunts, our candy shop, and the haunted house attraction that technically operated all year. The supernaturals that ran the old colonial style attraction did tend to go all out in

October, so it really was no wonder that tourism had increased substantially since the haunted house had opened its doors. I was going to have to see if Finn and Andre might want to make an evening of it. Well, as soon as Andre returned.

I'd also gotten a huge order for wedding favors, candles anointed with *Dreamtime Oil*, enough for every guest, and I'd had to really scramble, because that potion needed the full moon to work properly, so I'd had to have everything ready to go in advance.

The trouble with Andre grouping his shows together so he could be home in Haven Hollow more often and for longer stints, meant that he was really busy while he was away. We'd been trying to keep up with phone calls, even a couple video chats, but most of the time he'd either been working or sleeping. But finally, he was back in Portland and he only had two shows left, which meant he'd be home by the end of the week.

It was a little embarrassing, having butterflies in my stomach at my age, but I was just so happy that he was coming home. I knew Finn was looking forward to it, too.

Speaking of my teenager, he'd been a little grumpy for the past couple of weeks. Nothing hugely noticeable, but he was obviously in a mood. I couldn't tell if it was stress about getting his science fair project presentation ready in time, or if he was just missing Andre, or maybe it was just typical teenage boy stuff. All I did know was that he didn't want to talk about it. I'd asked him repeatedly if anything was going on, but I didn't want to press him too hard, figuring he'd eventually come to me if there was something I could do to help.

Now, it was finally the day of the science fair, and I'd closed the store early so I could be home when Finn got back from school. Whatever the outcome of his presentation, I wanted to celebrate by making him a special dinner. He'd put a lot of work into his project, and that deserved recognition, even if he hadn't won a ribbon (though I hoped he had). It was a bit of a bummer, but the science experiments hadn't been made available to parents and family, so I hadn't been able to watch Finn reveal his. I just hoped he'd want to tell me all about it.

That, combined with Andre coming home soon, would maybe help cheer him up a bit. Or at least, I hoped it would. I'd just slid the homemade pizza into the oven when the front door of the farmhouse opened and closed, and I heard the clatter of Finn dropping his backpack and kicking off his shoes.

"Hey, Mom," he caroled as he came down the hall. "What smells good?"

"Dinner." I grinned as he came through the door to the kitchen. "We're having mac n cheese pizza."

Which really sounded disgusting and wasn't exactly good in my mind, but it was Finn's favorite. "Really? That's awesome." He threw himself down into a chair at the old, heavy duty wooden table that dominated the kitchen. "Can I help?"

"It's all taken care of already, but thank you." So was the triple chocolate cake I'd baked earlier, but I'd keep hold of that surprise until later.

Cleaning up a few dishes in the sink gave me the opportunity to look Finn over. He seemed happy, and a lot lighter in mood than he had over the past few days. More like his old self, that was for sure. Maybe it really had been the science fair that was stressing him out, or missing Andre.

"So," I said slowly, as I washed up. "How did the science fair go?"

I didn't want to make him feel bad if it hadn't gone well, but Finn had put so much work into his project that I just couldn't see that happening. He'd been practically meeting up with Sophie at the school library every other night.

"Well." Finn dragged out the word, grinning

so wide, the freckles on his cheeks almost disappeared. “I got a runner up ribbon!”

He tugged the yellow ribbon out of his pocket, waving it in the air like a pennant.

“That’s great, buddy. Way to go!”

He was in a good enough mood that I risked it, and rising to my tip toes (because Finn now dwarfed me) I dropped a kiss on his cheek. It wasn’t that Finn wasn’t affectionate, it was just that he was getting older, and hugs and kisses from his mom were becoming more and more ‘uncool’. Though, he still let me get away with it most of the time with minimal grumbling, but only if his friends weren’t around to witness it.

Sure enough, he just smiled and accepted the hug before laying his ribbon on the table. “But do you want to know the coolest part?”

“Of course.”

“Sophie won first place!”

Trust Finn to be more excited about his friend’s success than his own. Pride welled up inside me, golden and glowing. I’d made mistakes in my life, messed up in a lot of ways, and sometimes even hurt people without meaning to. But Finn was hands down the best thing in my life. My biggest and best accomplishment, and just when I thought I couldn’t love him more, he proved me wrong.

“That’s amazing, good for her. She must

have been so happy."

Something flickered across Finn's face then, there and gone before I could fully understand what it was. Then his grin was back in full force.

"Yeah, she is." His eyes darted towards the oven. "How long until pizza?"

I laughed. Even with all the strange things in our lives, covens and faeries and magic and vampires, a teenage boy was still a bottomless pit when it came to food.

"Just a few more minutes. Then we can start on that one while the second one is cooking." His face lit up as I continued, "So, the judges liked your project?"

I finished washing up and dried my hands as we then sat down with our hot slices of pizza and I did my best to very inconspicuously shift most the mac n cheese off the top.

Finn took a big bite of his, chewing and swallowing before he answered, thank goodness. "Yeah, they did. But there was one guy who actually powered a little clock with a potato, and someone who made a really cool terrarium." He looked down at his ribbon. "Hence, runner up."

I chewed my own slice carefully, strands of mozzarella cheese stretching out. "And Sophie won first place. Good for her. The judges must have been really impressed."

That little flicker of something moved over Finn's face again, and he took a bigger bite. "Yeah, they did. Especially after Mr. Lannister left."

"Left?" I put my pizza down, confused. "Why would he leave? Isn't he the science teacher who was in charge of everything?"

Finn shrugged, his eyes on his slice. "I don't know why he left. I mean, he said something wasn't agreeing with him or his stomach or something, so the other judges filled in. After that, people's scores got a lot better."

Hmm. Mr. Lannister was a new teacher to Haven Hollow High. And he apparently was a pretty hard one. He might not have been Finn's favorite teacher, but he was good at what he did, from what I'd heard from other parents, anyway.

Finn was most of his way through a third slice of pizza by the time I'd started my second. He dabbed at the grease on his chin with a napkin and then served himself up another one, eyeing the mac n cheese on my plate with interest.

"You aren't going to eat your mac?"

"Have at it," I answered as I pushed the plate toward him.

"So," he glanced over towards the stove.

"You said something about a second pizza?"

I had to put my slice down, because I started laughing too hard to hold on to it.

***

I was just settling down at the kitchen table with my first coffee of the day early the next morning when my phone dinged with an alert from the council group chat.

The council had existed for as long as Haven Hollow had, with members joining and leaving as people moved and moved on. The council was meant to help protect the secrecy of the supernatural members of town, to allow them to live in peace with their mundane counterparts, and also with each other. The entire point of a Hollow was safety, so there was no infighting allowed. If one faction had a problem with another, they had to leave it at the proverbial gate and play nice.

I'd joined the council not long after moving to town, and I enjoyed helping out and pitching ideas. The constant meetings, though, were a bit draining, so eventually, I'd proposed the idea of a group chat. Finn had one all the time, for friends, group projects, events, and it had seemed like a good way to keep in contact without having to find a meeting place that was secure all the time.

Of course, we still needed a degree of secrecy, so we'd turned to Henner Tayir, our local Technomancer. Henner was the grandson of a witch (Betanya Tayir), and while he wasn't a witch or warlock himself, he'd inherited the gift of magical tech. That meant he could practically make any electronic device sit up and sing for him. Mostly he used his gift to build gadgets for his amateur ghost hunting business that he had with his friend R.J, and my ex-boyfriend, Marty, but he'd been happy to help us out. So, the council had ended up with a group chat that was secure enough that no one was going to be able to hack into it, even if they got ahold of one of our phones.

Still waking up, I tugged my phone closer and frowned at the message preview. It was from Roy, and it started off with a 'Very funny', which didn't exactly bode well for whatever came before.

Roy was Haven Hollow's resident Sasquatch, and he'd been on the council since I'd moved to town. We'd dated briefly, before I'd realized he had his own soulmate in Fifi, the succubus. It had stung, at first, but they were so happy together, and he and I wouldn't have worked long term, so I was just glad for him that he'd found his other half (and I was equally glad I'd found mine).

I knew Roy, and he wasn't the kind of man to use the council chat for sending funny pictures or anything, so something was up.

The message was a long one, and it was more of a rant, really.

Okay, whoever thought this was a good idea needs to smarten up. I spotted it on my way to work, and guess what? I wasn't the first person to see it. There were mundanes standing around taking pictures that I had to chase off.

I frowned, confused, but then I noticed that he'd included a couple pictures, so I opened one up and almost spit my coffee onto the table.

The images were obviously hastily taken from a smart phone, but the pictures were clear enough. Roy had gotten a shot of what looked like a shrub on the edge of someone's property, but the entire thing was made of gold.

"Crap and a half," I whispered to myself.

Chapter Four

The gold metal glinted in the sun, casting dazzling light across the grass.

There was no way the bush could have been made or cast, not with each of the leaves coated, every vein detailed in bright and shiny gold. Even the tiny blossoms that clung to it were gold, not to mention the dead buds. I very much doubted that someone would have such an expensive thing cast and then just planted it in the yard where anyone could damage it or steal it.

As I sat there, staring at the photos, my stomach sinking down somewhere close to my knees, another message dinged through from Roy.

Can someone ask Henner to scrub any photos or videos that ended up online while I deal with this? And Wanda, seriously, keep your people in line. We don't need this kind of crap right now.

I glanced over reflexively at my carefully arranged potion making equipment on the counter, chewing my lower lip. There was no way, right? I'd only made one *Gypsy Gold* potion, and Andre had taken it with him. I knew he had, because he'd told me about how the kids had loved it. He'd even sent me pictures of the kids with the items they'd turned into fool's gold.

And even if Andre hadn't taken the potion with him, even if he'd spilled it on a shrub or something and been too embarrassed to tell me, the potion only worked for an hour or so—an hour and a half max, depending on how much of the potion was used. And Andre had been gone for most of the month, so there was no way this gilded bush could have been from my potion.

But it was too close to be a coincidence, wasn't it?

Unless… my magic had been unstable lately, growing and changing into something new that I wasn't really familiar with, and definitely not comfortable with. But still, magic wasn't something that could be done accidentally, and definitely not without even noticing it.

I'd never heard of anyone casting spells in their sleep. And I didn't even know where that bush was so how could I have accidentally turned it into gold?

But what else could it have been? I guessed that Roy was technically right in that witches could have done such magic. But really, if they had, they would have done so with their own shrubs, and not left a fortune in gold on some random person's yard. And, furthermore, why would a witch want to turn a bush into gold? Especially when everyone was well aware that supernaturals in Haven Hollow needed to keep a low profile. It just didn't make any sense. And I was quite sure that as soon as Wanda read Roy's message, she wasn't going to be happy.

Sure enough, another message chimed, this time from an irritated Wanda.

Excuse me? It wasn't anyone in the coven, thanks. As if we have the time to go around turning random bushes into gold. That's completely ridiculous! I mean, really, Roy—maybe you should be looking for Rumpelstiltskin.

Roy replied fast enough that I was worried he was going to crack his phone screen.

Very funny, Wanda. Whoever the hell is responsible for this—I want them to know it's not funny. I just had to rip a three-hundred-pound bush out of the ground and then I had to hide it in my back yard so no more mundanes would see it.

Funny that you chose your own back yard for a gold bush that must be worth thousands, Wanda responded.

If you want it, come and get it, Roy texted back. *The point is that someone is screwing around with magic. Again. If you know someone else in town capable of creating this kind of magic, feel free to say so.*

Guilt chewed at me. I didn't know if I should say anything about my potion, or if it would just muddle things more. It really was too much to be a coincidence, that I dragged out an old potion recipe and something random turned to gold. But…

I squinted at the pictures Roy had sent again. It was hard to tell from a photo, but the gleam didn't look like Pyrite, which was pale and almost watery. That luster looked like real gold, and if the shrub was as heavy as Roy said it was, then that made sense, since real gold was ridiculously heavy. Pyrite wasn't.

There wasn't a potion I'd ever heard of that could turn something to gold, real gold, permanently. Or everyone who was anyone would have been doing it.

But I couldn't shed my nerves. Especially not since a couple months back, an entity with a grudge to settle had manipulated my own magic against me into a kind of bad luck curse. I'd thought that curse was gone—I mean, I hadn't seen any more signs of it recently, but what if it was still lingering? What if it had just gone dormant or something, and the curse was going to start causing problems for me and everyone in Haven Hollow again?

The blare of my phone jerked me out of my thoughts, the display announcing that it was a call from Wanda. She must have still been awake from the previous evening, to be calling this early.

Ever since Wanda had been accidentally blooded by her now husband, Lorcan Rowe, she'd been in kind of a precarious position. Being blooded by a vampire, who in his defense hadn't known she was a witch, only that she'd been in a bad car crash, had turned her into a Blood Witch, with some seriously scary powers. No one was a fan of Blood Witches, not the vampires, or the regular kind of witches, and they'd both been kind of up in arms about the situation.

They were pretty insistent that Lorcan finish the job and turn Wanda completely, but that would have stripped her of her magic, so no way was he doing it against her will. The solution had been an elaborate hoax where they tricked everyone into thinking Wanda was a full vampire, and that meant she'd had to take on a kind of permanent nocturnal schedule.

I answered before my phone could ring again, but I didn't even manage to get a hello out before Wanda started talking.

"What the spell crawled up Bigfoot's back-side?"

"I don't—"

"—and why the spell are we getting blamed for every magical mishap in town? Last time I checked, the coven members were the only people who actually knew what they were doing when it came to magic!"

"I'm sure—."

"—If Roy stubs his toe, blame the witches. If Stanley has the worst gas known to man, blame the witches. If those rotten teenagers cherry bomb Haven High's toilets, blame the witches! I'm so fed up with this crap!"

"Stanley had gas?"

She paused a moment. "Yeah, it was like a week ago—apparently, he wasn't paying attention when he was mixing up his sweet cream recipe and put too much of something in it which didn't agree with his centaur half and the result was the entirety of Main Street had to be evacuated because of the stench."

"What?"

She paused. "It was at night and you were already home with your Mr. Darcy."

"Oh."

I pulled my coffee mug a little closer to me, cupping it with my free hand. "To go back to this gold bush business, I think Roy's just frustrated—I don't think he meant to blame you."

"Well, it sure sounded like he meant to blame me and us."

"Try not to take offense."

"I swear, I would love to take that sasquatch down a peg or two."

"Wanda, don't get any ideas, please."

"Too late."

"Wanda..."

"Fine. I'm not going to do anything to Roy."

"Promisc?"

"Promise."

"Are you crossing your fingers?"

"Ugh, you're impossible to lie to."

I laughed. "The point is: this kind of thing could bring a lot of trouble for us, and Roy doesn't know much about magic."

"He knows jack-all about magic."

"Right. So, who else would he think of, other than Circle Scapegrace?"

Wanda sniffed, clearly not mollified at all. "And Taliyah's been harping at me about this, too. Can you believe that? Like I didn't grow out of random pranks a hundred years ago. Besides, if I could make a solid gold bush, it's not like I'd leave it in someone's yard! I'd keep it for myself and I wouldn't be making three-hundred-pound bushes either! I'd be making jewelry or something I could sell in my store."

"I believe you."

"I swear to the Goddess I'm going to hex that ape-man with jock itch."

My lips twitched, and I pressed them together to make sure I didn't laugh.

The phone crackled as she gave a gusty sigh. "Honestly, I haven't seen a witch hunt like this since the eighteen hundreds."

"Maybe it was just a fluke," I hedged, casting a worried look towards my potion making supplies. "An accident. The point is: I'm sure it will all blow over."

"If you think I'm letting this outrage, this, this, *profiling* go without an apology, you are very sadly mistaken, Poppy Morton."

Wanda was my BFF. I hadn't even known that friends like her could exist before I came to the Hollow. So, I closed my mouth and very carefully did not mention all the times that Wanda's Blood Witch powers had sparked out of control and she'd done something that most people agreed just couldn't be done. Like when she'd raised Libby, the zombie. Or when she'd brought Darla, a ghost, back to life and given her a physical body again. Or the time she and Maverick had accidentally turned a mannequin into a shapeshifter girl named Sybil who was currently living as Maverick's daughter.

Though, in Wanda's defense, her magical mishaps always seemed to revolve around bringing things to life, not turning living things into statues, gold or otherwise. Thank goodness it was just a bush—it would have been terrible if it had happened to a person or an animal.

"And I'm certainly not going to lend Roy my decades of experience and fantastically powerful magic and sheer brilliance until I've been appropriately groveled to, I can tell you that much," Wanda continued without pausing for breath. "I can't believe the nerve."

I didn't get a chance to make any kind of response, before I could hear a low male voice murmuring too quietly for me to make out the words.

Wanda cleared her throat. "I have to go. Lorcan just offered to make things up to me, which means really naughty sex."

"Oh, God, Wanda, I could have done without that."

"Once you start getting some from your Mr. Darcy, you'll understand what I mean."

"Thanks for that." Yes, I'd talked about my

sex life, or lack thereof, with Wanda. And she'd told me, just like I'd known she would, that I was wasting time and I should 'jump Mr. Darcy's bones before he realizes you're not Elizabeth Bennett'. Thanks, Wanda.

"I'll talk to you later, Poppy."

And then she was gone.

I had to laugh a little. It was nice to see Wanda so happy with Lorcan. They'd had a really rough road to get to where they now were, and they deserved to be happy. But still, if Wanda hadn't turned the shrub to gold, and none of the other coven members had done it, then who had? And why? It seemed to me to be the strangest of pranks.

Finn stumbled into the kitchen then, rubbing his bleary eyes, his blonde hair, so like mine, sticking up in places. He yawned, wide enough to make his jaw crack. "Who were you talking to?"

"Wanda." I stood up and went to the fridge to grab the orange juice for him as something occurred to me—even if it was still a longshot. "Hey, Finn, you didn't touch any of my potion making equipment, did you?"

He blinked at me, frowning. "No. Why?"

That was what I figured, but I sighed anyway. "No reason, just curious." I didn't want to overwhelm him first thing in the morning by explaining what was going on with the golden bush. And I also didn't want him to get any ideas about getting involved, because that's exactly what he did whenever he got an inkling of something going down in this town—he wanted to get involved. And I very definitely did not want him to get involved.

He smiled at me sleepily as I passed him the orange juice and went to prepare him some cereal, and I smiled back automatically.

As to Finn playing around with my potion making equipment, I didn't think he would have. He didn't know how to make potions—and he'd never been much interested in making them or even watching me make them. Furthermore, I'd only made the one *Gypsy Gold* potion, anyway. And, I reminded myself, that potion was with Andre. I made a mental note to call Andre later, and make sure he still had his bottle with him. Which was a silly thought, because what—his bottle just decided to take the next train back to Haven Hollow? Yeah, ridiculous.

The point was, I just didn't know what was going on in Haven Hollow. With any luck, this gold bush business was just a fluke. The kind of magical hiccup that happened in a town with a significant paranormal population—with magic practically in the air.

Yes, this would all blow over and turn out to be nothing at all.

But the sinking feeling in my gut told me I didn't really believe that.

Chapter Five

Hallowed Homes Realty was the number one place in Haven Hollow for people (mundanes or supernaturals) looking for a home that suited their needs. Even if their needs ran more along '*cemetery with consecrated ground and a crypt*' than '*would really like a third bathroom*'.

When I'd moved to town, the real estate market had been run by Ophelia, the Night Hag's, iron fist, and she'd been very particular about who she let live in the town. She hadn't liked humans at all, but I'd had magic at least, so she'd allowed me to buy my old farm house. She'd also run the council at the time.

Then she'd made the very poor decision to try and kill Wanda, and ended up a statue out on Wanda's front lawn. Of course, that hadn't been a magical mishap, but it had been a very deliberate choice on Wanda's part. Apparently, she was into Night Hag lawn art. Who knew?

Ever since that day, Fifi had taken over as premier realtor in town, and she was doing amazing things with Hallowed Homes. Even the offices themselves were different: no longer the cold, stagnant, austere building with uncomfortable chairs. Instead, it was a gorgeously decorated office space with potted plants, and a little waterfall fountain, and leather conference room chairs that sighed and molded around a person.

As a supernatural meeting space with lots of room to sit and a big table, Fifi graciously let the Haven Hollow council host many of our meetings at Hallowed Homes. The Half-Moon Bar and Grill up the road from my shop was the other popular spot, since Roy owned it, but it was a restaurant that catered to humans too, and sometimes it could be tricky making sure no one overheard something they shouldn't.

I settled into my chair and sat back to wait for the others to arrive for the council meeting, and checked my phone. I had a text from Finn to tell me that he'd gotten to Marty's safely, and that he and RJ and Henner were planning a night of video games. I slipped my cell back in my pocket with a soft smile. Marty was the first friend I'd made in Haven Hollow, and one of the best friends I'd ever had. That was why I'd gone along with it when he'd asked me out, thinking that maybe my love for my friend could turn into something a bit more passionate.

And at the beginning, I had felt something for Marty that I'd thought was romance. I'd been attracted to him and I'd thought maybe we could have a future together, but soon those feeling had switched—they'd changed to simple platonic feelings and I'd never been able to get any semblance of romantic feelings for him again.

The truth of the matter was that I'd let things between us go on for way too long, afraid I didn't know my own heart. But, in the end, I'd just ended up hurting him, and for a while, I'd thought he'd never forgive mc. But things were slowly getting better between us, and we were finally able to smile at one another in passing (before we wouldn't even be 'in passing' because I was fairly convinced he'd been doing everything in his power to avoid me). We still weren't to the point of hanging out and maybe we never would be again, but I hoped one day we could. Of course, it only further complicated matters that I was now with Andre, and very publicly at that. It was my absolute hope that Marty would find his special person soon—someone who could love him in the same way he loved them. It really meant the world to me that he'd kept up his friendship with Finn—that showed just what a great man Marty was, even if he wasn't the man for me.

Fifi was bustling around, setting out coffee and cream in the middle of the conference table, looking amazing in her black pencil skirt and red silk blouse. With her centerfold figure and her long, platinum hair pulled up into a bun, it would have been easy to be a bit self-conscious around Fifi, but she was just so nice, that it made it impossible.

Roy stomped in a few minutes later, clearly still in a bad mood from the scowl on his face. He ducked to get through the conference room door, growling something that sounded a lot like 'damned witches', but I couldn't be sure. The second he caught sight of Fifi, though, his shoulders softened, the harsh lines of his frown eased up, and he bent down far enough to give her a small kiss. And I was happy to report that there was no part of me that felt in the least bit jealous or uncomfortable. Actually, I felt the opposite—more than happy that they'd found each other, even if seeing them did make me yearn for my own man.

My own man.

Even the words still seemed foreign in my head, and I couldn't help the way a smile stole my lips as soon as an image of Andre shaped itself in my head. Maybe Wanda was right, and I needed to stop waiting and jump his bones the second I got the chance?

I fought back a sigh and the burning desire that alighted within me whenever I pictured Andre's face or imagined his deep voice. He'd be home in a few more days and then I could hold him and kiss him and maybe do more with him.

I swallowed hard at that thought.

Not long after Roy walked in, Police Chief Taliyah Morgan entered, and since it was only supernaturals present, she didn't bother keeping up the glamour that made her look human. Taliyah was also Princess Olwen of the Winter court of Faerie, but it was better not to use that name around her. She'd only recently found out about her heritage, and she was still adjusting to it all.

Taliyah's fae nature made sure that she was flawlessly gorgeous as she came into the room, pale skin, frost white hair, ever so slightly pointed ears, with every mark or wrinkle she'd earned over a human lifetime wiped away like they had never been. It didn't hide the dark bruises under her eyes, though. She looked tired.

Fifi's brother, Angelo, showed up next, looking devastating in his black suit and red shirt with no tie. He flashed his killer smile around the room before taking a seat, and I really hoped he was here to help get things done, and not to just be a general nuisance to Fifi like he usually was. Of course, I did have to admit that ever since Lydia had entered his life, he'd shown a side of himself no one had ever thought he had—a potentially caring side. Now, I didn't know anything about the two of them or if something was going on between them or not, so I could have been making the whole thing up, but I was fairly sure there was something different about Angelo and I had a mind that Lydia had everything to do with it.

Wanda showed up about fifteen minutes later, strutting through the door like a runway model, a to-go coffee cup in her hand. Fifi had just finished work, so I got why she was all dolled up. But Wanda had probably just rolled out of bed, so her maroon sweater dress with black leather boots was probably meant more as a statement. I didn't miss the scowl she sent in Roy's direction and neither did he.

Lorcan stepped into the room after her, nodding to everyone gathered, his blonde hair looking a bit windswept for some reason. Wanda took the seat next to mine, with Lorcan on the other side, while Roy glowered in their general direction.

I slumped down into my seat, because I could already tell the meeting wasn't going to go well. Officially, we'd all come together to discuss the huge amounts of turnover in residents the town was seeing. Hollows were supposed to be safe places, where all the political problems of the greater world were left at the door, and the magical people who wanted to live in peace next to their human neighbors could do just that. Unfortunately, Haven Hollow hadn't exactly been living up to those ideals lately.

In fact, ever since I'd moved to town, it seemed like it had just been one thing after another. Faeries kidnapping kids, serial killers who traveled through mirrors, fights between covens, civil wars in Winter, vengeful furies, and murderous vampires. And with things heating up between the witches and the vampires again, it was starting to look like there might be another Blood War on the horizon—something we needed like a hole in the head. The gist of the matter was that no one felt like Haven Hollow was the safe place it was meant to be.

So, they were leaving in droves, heading for new Hollows that were being formed around the country. Even humans (who had no idea about the supernatural) were moving away from Haven Hollow, looking for more peaceful places.

The whole situation meant that the council was getting a lot of petitions from supernaturals wanting to move to Haven Hollow, since there was now obviously space for them. The trouble was sorting through those petitions and weeding out those who wouldn't have been approved for other Hollows, due to their more colorful pasts. The last thing we wanted was a bunch of misfit miscreants with magic. Wow, that was a lot of Ms.

It felt like sorting through a lot of resumes, trying to see who would be a good fit, or who wouldn't clash with the people already living in town, or at least who wouldn't probably kick off the next disaster. After a couple hours of debating and bickering really, everyone was tired and cranky, and the tension just kept winding tighter and tighter until I wanted to run out of the room.

It finally came to a head when Wanda negligently tossed an application back onto the table, letting it drift back and forth before sliding halfway towards the 'no' pile.

"Pass," she said, taking a sip of her probably cold latte. "I've met her. I wouldn't let her onto my lawn, never mind into my coven."

Roy slammed the paper he'd been reading down onto the table, his jaw clenched so tightly,

I could see the muscles jumping. "Wanda, do you think you could take something seriously for once?"

Everything went still then. I could hear Fifi's surprised little inhale from the head of the table. Wanda, meanwhile, took an obnoxiously long slurp from her drink. There was a dangerous gleam in her eyes that made the back of my neck prickle. Lorcan had the copy of that dangerous look and when he cleared his throat and leaned forward, clearly ready to battle with Roy, Wanda placed a hand on his and shook her head. Then she faced Roy with a smile that could have killed.

"Please, Roy," she said way, way too pleasantly. "What exactly am I not taking seriously?"

Paper crinkled as the sheet in Roy's hands started to tear before he let it go. "This is actually serious. It's important for the safety of the town. It's not about you getting to swipe left on someone just because you don't like their clothes."

"When did I say I didn't like her... clothing?" she asked, eyes narrowing. Wanda didn't scream. Instead, she got this look on her face that was far scarier. "But now that you mention it—yes—cotton and polyester blend, that's the reason I want her banned." Wanda smiled, but the skin around her eyes was tight.

"You know what I mean," Roy growled.

She shook her head. "My voting Dierdre Recktish out definitely doesn't have anything to do with the fact that she failed to mention that she'd been kicked out of three covens already for seriously injuring people she decided were her rivals. But let's talk about fashion instead."

That at least took a bit of the wind out of Roy's sails, but he swiped a hand back through his close-cropped dark hair and pushed on. "I'm just saying, this is the worst possible time for little magical pranks like turning bushes into gold—or other things that might attract attention from the mundanes. If we can't keep the supernatural under wraps here, do you think people are going to want to live in Haven Hollow? The whole town will collapse if it doesn't have residents. The whole Hollow might be at risk."

Technically, the speech was for the entire table, but even I noticed that it seemed to be mostly aimed in Wanda's direction. From the way her purple tipped fingers curled into her hands, she'd noticed it too.

"As I already told you," she said through her teeth, her smile now more of a snarl. "It wasn't me who turned the bush into gold. Nor was it any of my friends, or anyone in the coven. So lay off, Roy, and try being grateful for your very expensive houseplant."

Roy scowled at her, his heavy brows pulling down until they almost touched over the bridge of his nose. "And if it were you or one of your own who did it? Am I supposed to believe that you'd out yourself? Or any of your coven would?"

"Listen, you unmagical lumberjack," Wanda snarled, leaning forward.

"Um, actually…" I had to fight not to raise my hand like I was back in middle school or something. "I think I might... well, possibly... I don't know actually, but... well, maybe I might possibly know what caused it."

"Start 'splainin', Lucy," Wanda said, giving me a pointed eyebrow.

There were a lot of eyes on me all of a sudden and none of them were very happy.

I took a deep breath. "Well, a couple of weeks ago, I made a potion called *Gypsy Gold.* And, well, it's kind of a flashy, showy potion, that doesn't have much of a use, really. It's actually just used for impressing people, honestly."

"What does it do?" Roy growled.

"Don't you dare growl at Poppy!" Wanda yelled at him, narrowing her eyes. "Unless you'd really like to see some witch magic in action."

"I apologize, Poppy," Roy said, not bothering to acknowledge Wanda at all. "Please go on."

I felt myself sliding further down the seat. "What does it do?" I repeated his question, feeling like my stomach was now in my feet. "Well, that's the, uh, the interesting part." Then I let out this strange laugh and Wanda gave me a look that told me to get ahold of myself. "It... well, it turns whatever it's applied to into... well, into *Fool's* Gold—not real gold, of course. And it only turns objects into Fool's Gold only for an hour or so. Not like... well, not like anything longer than that." I finished with that weird little laugh again.

Roy scowled. "And you're just bringing this up now?"

I lifted my hands and shrugged. "Well, I honestly don't think the two situations are anything but a coincidence. I mean—there's no way *Gypsy Gold* could do what's happened to the bush."

"Turn it to gold?" Roy said, frowning even more deeply.

"Yes, it couldn't. I mean—I only made one bottle! And one bottle isn't nearly enough to cover an entire bush! And not only that, but I gave the one bottle I made to Andre when he left town for his show."

"Then you don't even have it any longer?" Roy asked.

I shook my head. "No! Andre has it and he's in Portland and has been for weeks!"

"Could someone else have gotten their hands on the recipe?" Roy asked.

I shook my head again. "There's literally no way that could have happened, unless the person was invisible and took notes while I was making it. Not only that, but *Gypsy Gold* is only good for an hour at the most!"

Angelo frowned up at the ceiling from where he was half reclined into his chair. "Don't you have a kid?"

I frowned at him, fighting the urge to remind him that he very well knew Finn's name. "Yes," I said and none too friendly, not appreciating him trying to involve Finn in this.

"Could he have taken the potion and painted the bush with it?" Angelo continued, sounding bored. "That sounds like something a kid would want to do."

"Paint a bush?" Wanda asked, scowling at the demon. "Clearly, you don't know any kids and you obviously don't know Finn."

"Then he wouldn't want to paint the bush?" Angelo asked, as if he wanted to be sure he understood her.

"No! He's fourteen, you lout!" Wanda answered.

"Finn isn't interested in potions," Lorcan continued, as Wanda continued shaking her head like everyone else in the room was an idiot.

"Like Lorcan said, Finn isn't interested in potions and nor does he know how to make them," I added as I looked around the room, wanting everyone to keep Finn out of this.

"So—" Roy started, but one look shut him up.

"I asked him if he'd touched any of my brewing equipment and he said 'no'."

"The gold bush wasn't caused by Poppy's potion or by Finn," Wanda continued, glaring at anyone who dared to look at her. "That potion is currently with Mr. Darcy in Portland and the effects only last an hour. Now let's move on and stop putting this on Poppy. The poor thing already looks like she's going to pass out from all the stress you're putting on her." Then her attention settled on Roy.

"I apologize if we're stressing you out, Poppy," Roy amended.

"It's okay," I managed with a small sigh as I then smiled to Wanda who just nodded at me in a way that told me '*I've got your back.*'

"You said your potion only turns things to gold for an hour?" Taliyah had her police look on. Her eyes narrowed slightly as she turned the facts over in her head, looking at them from every angle.

"Right. Plus or minus maybe ten minutes."

She faced Roy. "That bush has been gold for hours now."

"Gold is still gold," Roy grumbled.

"Haven't we been over this?" Wanda muttered.

"Well, that's the other thing," I pointed out. "My potion isn't actually real gold. It's pyrite—fool's gold, not real at all."

"And that bush is real gold," Taliyah continued.

Roy nodded. "I can bend the stuff with my fingers. Whatever turned it, it's not some party trick. It's real magic—not a potion."

"Right." I chewed my lower lip thinking.

"So, it isn't exactly the same thing," Angelo answered on a shrug. "But it's kind of too much of a coincidence that Poppy literally just brewed the potion and then this bush shows up?"

Wanda looked at him, frowning. "Didn't we vote you off the council? What are you still doing here?"

"He got voted back in after the good deed he did for Lydia," Roy answered, absently waving Wanda's question away.

"Right. What he said," Angelo answered,

sounding very haughty.

Taliyah tapped her stack of papers against the table, looking thoroughly done with everything. "A gold bush is the least of my concerns at the moment. There's enough going on in this town that I don't even want to waste my time with this. Especially when I'm dealing with a rash of petty thefts all over town."

"Thefts?" I repeated.

"What's been stolen?" Lorcan asked.

Taliyah shrugged. "We've been getting calls for all kinds of stuff that's gone missing—jewelry, dishes, Christmas ornaments. And that's just the most recent stuff that's gone missing in the last few hours."

Angelo, who was slumped back in his chair with his hands folded over his stomach, and who I'd honestly thought was now taking a nap, spoke up, his voice beyond bored. "It's probably just kids pulling pranks."

"Theft isn't a prank," Taliyah snapped.

"And neither is drawing attention to magic," Roy said, his comment very much directed at Wanda.

I winced as Wanda stood, her chair rolling back into the wall behind her. "I told you, you ape man, the bush prank wasn't the coven. And good luck turning the stupid thing back into a live plant without the aid of any witches, because if you think I'm going to help you after sitting through this crap, you're dumber than you look."

And then she was gone, stalking out the door with Lorcan at her heels. The vampire cast a glare back over his shoulder at Roy before following her out. I was sure he'd pay Roy a visit later—the two had never gotten along.

Annoyed, and feeling bad for Wanda getting ganged up on, I shot a reproachful look around the table. "Wanda's magic might be unpredictable," I admitted. "But she isn't a liar. If she says it wasn't her or the other witches in Scapegrace, then it wasn't."

We tried to soldier on after that, to look through more applications and get some things done. But the mood had very much soured, and we only lasted another twenty minutes before we all decided to throw in the towel and try again another night.

I headed home for the evening, and I couldn't help but think the streets felt a little darker and colder than usual.

Chapter Six

I finished the last layer of noodles in the lasagna and carefully sprinkled a few handfuls of cheese on top of it all.

Finn was beside me, helping to throw together everything we'd need for a side salad with more enthusiasm than skill. Now all we needed to do was put the pan in the oven and let it cook until it turned into a whole lot of cheesy, saucy goodness.

Andre was finally home and coming over for dinner, and I wasn't sure who was more excited, Finn or me. Finn had even volunteered to help me put dinner together, something he never did. Now, all that was left was to get the garlic bread together for a quick toast in order to pair it with the lasagna when it came out of the oven.

I was in the process of looking for a brush for the garlic butter in one of the cupboards when I realized one of my measuring cups (dedicated only to potions) was in the wrong spot. While I did both cooking and potion making in the kitchen, I had different utensils for both, and I kept them carefully separate. Potions were meant to be worn on the skin, not eaten, so it was important to have separate tools.

I wasn't always the most organized person, but I was pretty militant about that one rule—potion equipment in the far left cupboard and regular baking equipment on the right. I wasn't about to risk Finn's and my health by using the wrong spoon or bowl. So, finding the measuring cup, the purple one I only used for potions, in the wrong cupboard was definitely worrying.

"Mom, should I put the dressing on now? Or wait?"

Finn's question jerked my attention away, and I closed the cabinet door. "Oh, no, we'll wait until closer to dinner. We don't want the lettuce to get all soggy."

"Okay," he said, fidgeting a little with the bottle.

He'd been distracted ever since he came home from school, and I'd just chalked that distraction up to him being excited about Andre finally being back, but I was starting to think it might be something else. Finn didn't usually get distracted so easily.

I gave him a gentle hip check. "What's up? You seem to be thinking pretty hard about something."

He gave me a wilted version of his usual sunny smile. "I'm good. Just thinking about school stuff. No biggie."

I nodded and started brushing the garlic butter on the loaf of French bread that I'd cut in half earlier. "Anything in particular on your mind? Maybe I could help?"

Finn fiddled with the salad bowl, turning it back and forth like it was a worry stone. "Nah. I'm good. It's nothing."

Now, I didn't have my son's supernatural ability to tell when someone was lying to me. But I'd given birth to Finn, so my mother senses were definitely tingling. Before I could ask him anything more though, there was a knock on the front door, and Finn's whole face lit up.

"Andre's here!"

And then he was blazing through the house like a comet, and all I could do was laugh as I trailed along in his wake.

***

Dinner had turned out pretty darn well, if I did say so myself. Even Finn had been focused on eating instead of playing with Ouire or peppering Andre with a million questions. Instead, the three of us happily munched on salad, garlic bread, and lasagna, while Finn washed it down with a Sprite, Andre with a glass of red wine, and me with an iced tea.

I'd pulled up a chair for Ouire to sit on, with the understanding that he was to keep his pages off the table. I didn't want to risk him getting tomato sauce on himself, because I had no idea how you would ever clean a magical book. There was probably a Magician spell for it.

With everything else going on, I hadn't had time to make a cake or an elaborate dessert, but Andre and Finn seemed to appreciate the chocolate chip cookies I'd baked, so I considered it a win. When the food was gone, Finn finally launched into asking Andre about the shows he'd done, and Andre was happy to answer him. And I was beyond happy to sit there, sipping at my after-dinner tea, as I listened to them both, their voices washing over me like a balm, soothing some of the tension from my neck and shoulders.

"And, oh, Poppy, you should have seen the birthday girl's face when I turned a garden stone to gold with your potion." Andre laughed, a low, rich sound. "I thought her eyes were going to pop out of her head."

"I'm so happy to hear that!"

"Then the kids liked Mom's potion?" Finn asked excitedly.

Andre nodded as he smiled at me. "I reckon they rather loved it. I actually purchased a few bits of Pyrite from a gem shop, so with a little sleight of hand, the children got to keep their 'gold treasures' from the party."

I laughed, imagining it. That was the kind of magic I liked best, the kind that brought laughter and joy and made lives a little better.

"And then," Andre said, leaning forward like he was telling us a secret. His blue eyes were dancing, the corners of his lips twitching. "Then one of the birthday girl's guests walked up to me, really quite solemn. She tugged at my sleeve and said, 'Excuse me, Mister Magician. But can you turn my brother into a kitten?'"

Finn was hysterical at that and Ouire began bounding around the table, as if echoing Finn's jubilance. The evening had turned out just as lovely as I'd hoped it would, and everything felt right with Andre back with us.

An hour or so later, though, I couldn't help but notice that Finn's smile was a bit strained.

"Finn? Is everything okay, buddy?"

His head jerked up at my question, a slightly guilty look on his face. “Oh, yeah Mom. I’m good.”

Andre raised a brow in my direction, as if to say he’d noticed Finn acting strangely as well and, in response, all I could do was shrug as subtly as I could so Finn wouldn’t notice. I wasn’t sure what was wrong with Finn, but something definitely was. It was the same expression he’d been wearing earlier, before Andre had returned. I loved being a mom, and Finn was the most important part of my life, but it felt really good to know there was someone else looking out for him, someone else who would try to coax out any problems he might have been having.

By the time all the cookies were gone, Finn was mostly back to his usual sunny self and he’d decided to work off his dinner by destroying zombies in his newest video game. Andre and I, meanwhile, retired to the living room for an after dinner coffee. While I was in the kitchen, pouring our second round, I heard Finn walk into the living room.

“Andre?” he asked.

“Yes?” Andre prompted.

I quietly walked to the wall separating the living room from the kitchen and watched Finn chew his lower lip, obviously thinking hard. Finally, he blurted out in a rush, "Is it possible to undo a spell?"

Andre's brow wrinkled, and he slowly lowered his cup back to its saucer. "What do you mean?"

His gaze solidly on Ouire, who was standing beside him, Finn stroked a hand along the book's spine. "Well, once you've cast a spell, and it's out in the world, can you uncast it? Cancel it out? That kind of thing."

Andre gave the question some thought. "I don't know. I suppose it depends on what type of magic is used," he said slowly. "As far as I know, once cast, the spell exists separate from the one who cast it. And, a Magician's spells are meant to bring hope to people, so I've never really thought about how you'd go about undoing them."

That clearly wasn't the answer he was looking for, going by the way Finn's face dropped.

"Why do you ask?" I said as I walked back into the living room, carrying two cups of coffee.

"Oh, I was just curious," Finn answered, rather evasively. "I was just thinking about some of the spells the coven does and I just wondered if they could ever undo them."

"I imagine Wanda could," I said as I cocked my head to the side and thought about it. "Or maybe she'd just create another spell to cancel the first one?"

"Could we do the same?" Finn asked Andre. "With our Magician magic?"

"You mean like a Magicless spell?" Andre asked.

I fought back a shudder at the mention of the dark magicians. While Magicians like Finn and Andre used their powers to bring hope to people and make the world a better place, their evil counterpart, the Magicless, were those who had lost all hope and allowed it to make them bitter and cruel. One had infiltrated Finn's school, attempting to break him and turn him dark too, but we'd managed to stop her.

"No, nothing like that." Flustered, Finn took a deep breath.

"Is everything okay, Finn?" I asked.

He looked at me and nodded. "It's pretty late, Mom. I should probably go to bed."

"Where is my son and what have you done with him?" I asked on a laugh, because Finn never willingly went to bed on time. He was always begging me for one more hour.

He gave me a quick smile and then started for the stairs, before turning around and calling out, "Goodnight, Andre. Night, Mom."

Ouire's tail drooped, and I blinked in surprise as Finn's feet disappeared up the stairs.

Andre turned back to me, concerned. "Is everything alright? Did I say something to upset him?"

"I don't think so. He's been gushing nonstop this whole week about you coming home." I squeezed Andre's shoulder as I slipped past him. "I'm just going to go check on him. I'll be right back."

His smile had all the reassurance I needed. "Of course."

Finn was changed, with teeth and hair brushed and all ready for bed by the time I made it up the stairs to his bedroom. He'd just slipped under the covers, and tugged them up to his chin like he used to when he was just a little guy, when he'd had a bad dream and wanted to hide.

"Hey, pookey," I said, calling him by his childhood nickname, as I padded softly across the room. "I just wanted to say goodnight and tuck you in."

He was tense, his narrow shoulders rigid beneath his sheets. "I'm too old to be tucked in."

"Too old?" I hummed like I was considering it while I smoothed out his comforter and sat on the edge of his bed. "I might agree to that in a few years. Let's say when you're thirty-five."

"Thirty-five? That's way more than a few years!"

I laughed. “You can tuck yourself in then, but in the meantime, it’s my job. Deal?”

He rolled his eyes at me, but at least he was smiling and looked a bit more relaxed. I just sat on his bed for another few seconds, allowing the quiet to echo between us, before I played the part of concerned mom. “Finn. Is everything alright? You don’t seem yourself lately.”

He started chewing his lower lip, and I had to stomp down my instinct to tell him to stop. Something was clearly bothering him, but he didn’t seem to want to bring it up. Pushing wasn’t the way, I knew that. It would just irritate him, or make him defensive, but I had to ask yet again. I hated to see him struggling with something.

I smoothed his hair back from his forehead with my palm. “You know you can talk to me, right? You can tell me anything.”

Finn closed his eyes and took a deep breath that shuddered on the way in. He smiled at me when he opened his eyes again, going for reassuring but not quite getting there. “Nothing’s wrong, Mom. Everything is fine. I just have a heavy load at school and some of my classes are stressing me out a little.”

“Okay,” I said, trying not to show how worried I was. “Well, if you need help, you’ll let me know?”

"I don't know that you'll be able to help me with my algebra, Mom," he said on a laugh.

"Okay, so maybe go to Andre for that, but I can help you with everything else," I answered on a laugh. "Anyway... sleep tight, buddy, and... don't let the bedbugs bite!" Then I reached out and tickled him and he gave me a look like he wasn't impressed.

"Mom, I'm seriously way too old for tickling."

"Oh, excuse me!" I said, feigning affront. I stood up and pretended to leave but then rounded on him and, grabbing his foot, tickled the bottom of it as he erupted into laughter.

"Okay, Mom!" he called out in between peals of laughter. "Uncle, Mom! Uncle!"

I released his foot then, and he immediately pulled it back under the covers as he smiled up at me.

"Goodnight, Finn," I said as I pressed my luck and kissed his forehead. Finn gave a sleepy, good-natured grumble, and when I hit the light switch on my way out of the room, I looked back, only to find him smiling at me.

Chapter Seven

Even with worry for Finn hanging over my head like a little dark rain cloud, I couldn't help but be in a great mood the next day.

Andre had remained after dinner, helping me clean up plates and glasses, before giving me a very sweet kiss at the door as he headed home for the evening. It had left me all rosy warm and humming inside for the rest of the night. And, yes, I'd debated asking him to stay for the night, but somehow it didn't feel right yet. And I didn't want to rush things. I wanted to cherish the experience of each step of our courtship (such an old-fashioned word, but that's what it felt like between the two of us). I wanted to savor each little step, never feeling as if I'd rushed any part of it.

Finn had been a bit subdued when I'd dropped him off at school in the morning, but he'd still chatted happily about his friends and some plans they were working on. And he was still clearly thrilled that Andre was back, so whatever his problem was, it probably didn't have to do with Andre. Maybe it was nothing more than just school stress. I hoped that was all it was.

Maybe after I closed the store for the night, I'd take Finn to Stomper's Creamery for an ice cream sundae to see if I could coax out whatever was upsetting him. Everything went down better with ice cream, and with the cooler weather, the place wasn't usually packed like it was in the summer months, so we'd have a bit of privacy.

Things were hopping at Poppy's Potions, so at least I didn't have much time to dwell on the worry gnawing at my gut. I was too busy helping customers, refilling stock, and taking inventory of my supplies.

It wasn't just my store, either, that was going through a major bump in business. All of Main Street seemed to have a crowd filing in and out, and not just the stores and restaurants. The street itself was packed, to the point that auto traffic was backing up.

It was a bit early still for these kinds of

tourist crowds—Halloween was still weeks away, but maybe the town had some kind of event going on that I hadn't heard about? I'd been pretty busy, so unless it was a council planned event, I'd probably missed it.

There wasn't any time to dwell on it, as I had customers to see to, including a woman a few years older than I was in a tuxedo cat sweater with lime green framed glasses, who seemed to be trying to buy out my entire stock. Multiple potions filled her basket along with twelve or so dreamcatchers and the biggest beeswax candles already anointed for dreams and pleasant sleep. She was going to town, and I was quite happy to help her do it.

When she finally ran out of steam, and possibly breath, she plonked the two wicker baskets down on the counter with a wide grin. I reached behind the counter to retrieve the other two she'd left there for safe keeping. All were to the point of overflowing.

My own grin was pretty wide as I plugged each purchase into my ancient cash register. My potions weren't exactly pricey. Wanda constantly berated me for undervaluing them and myself, but this woman was still purchasing more than any single person ever had—as in, she was buying them by the armload. And that meant the relatively frugal cost of each added up quickly, especially when paired with the pillar candles and the dreamcatchers.

There was a happy chirp in my voice when I gave the customer the total.

"Okay, how does this work?" She fished around in her pocket for a bit. "I give you these, and you can make change?"

I blinked. "I'm sorry?"

"Here," she said happily, laying out three gold-coated leaves on my counter—like something you might wear on a chain as a necklace.

Now, I'd had some very interesting attempts at bartering as a way to pay for my potions in the past, especially from some of the older supernatural types in the Hollow who just couldn't seem to grasp a fungible economy. Fae could be the worst, and once I'd been offered a pure white cow for some candles. What would I even do with a cow? Thank goodness Finn hadn't found out about that one.

Gold leaves were a first, though.

I wasn't insulted. I'd had some argumentative tourists in the past, who'd come in skeptics, not believing what my potions could do. This particular lady didn't seem to be one of them, though. She seemed genuinely delighted with everything in my shop, so it was hard to get in a snit over it. The other reason this whole situation didn't make me angry, was because all three leaves were made out of solid gold.

They were beautiful, with every scalloped edge on the leaf done perfectly. The stems, the veins, they looked like they could have just been plucked off a tree. The light above cast them with a satiny sheen, but the one strange thing I noticed was that there was no loop on any of them that would allow for hanging them from a necklace.

So, of course, I could only wonder one thing—was this another case along the lines of the gold bush that had randomly appeared in someone's yard? Big red alarm bells suddenly started clanging away in my head.

I looked up at the woman. "Where on earth did you get these?"

She blinked, her smile faltering. "Oh. Off the tree up the road."

"The tree up the road?" I frowned.

She nodded excitedly. "It's a gold tree! And there's a crowd around it a mile thick, seems like! I could only get close enough to grab these three leaves and I had to push my way through everyone just to do that." Then she took a breath as my heart plummeted down to my feet. A gold tree? Roy wasn't going to like this—not one bit. "We all figured it was a stunt Haven Hollow did for tourists?"

"A stunt?"

She nodded again. "You know, like coupons to use in town? But gold leaves instead of paper?"

A whole tree turned into gold? She was kidding, right? I could only hope she was kidding. Especially right out on Main Street, the busiest road in the entire Hollow. But the woman only looked at me like I was the one who wasn't in the know.

"Um, well, I had no idea there was a gold tree in town."

Her face fell. "Oh. That's too bad."

I didn't want her walking out the door with those leaves. Plus, I needed to close the shop asap and get out there to see what in the world was going on. So, although it would hurt my pocketbook a bit (actually, maybe it wouldn't—all depending on what the gold leaves might be worth), I plastered a big smile onto my face.

"But you know what? I'll honor the leaf coupons for you."

"Oh, you will?" she crowed, snatching up the handle of the basket like she was worried I'd change my mind.

"Yes, whatever marketing stunt the mayor is working on by bringing that tree to town, he simply forgot to inform me, but there's always something fun brewing in this town."

She nodded excitedly again. "This town is

wonderful. Always so exciting. It's the best place, especially during October. I'll have to come back again next year! Hopefully he'll bring the gold tree back! It's really the best idea to get tourists excited to come to your town!"

I kept my smile in place while she bustled off, and then I ran to the door, flipping the sign to closed before locking up.

It wasn't hard to find the tree. All I had to do was follow the throngs of people who were swimming like a school of fish up Main Street. When I found the tree, I noticed the lady in my store had been correct—there was now a multitude of onlookers crowding around it, pushing each other to get closer, taking pictures, and, oh goodness, taking videos of themselves with the tree. Roy was going to have a fit and this time it was going to be legendary, if he hadn't already had one.

All but the leaves at the very tippy top of the tree had been stripped, with people trying to bend smaller branches off, and even picking at the bark, but to no avail. To all appearances, the whole tree was solid gold.

My heart was slamming inside my chest, bruising up against the inside of my ribs. This was bad, very bad. Places like Haven Hollow existed to keep the supernatural hidden, and safe away from prying human eyes. And because supernaturals were already leaving Haven Hollow, something like this—well, it could only make matters worse. Way worse. Something this obvious and flashy would continue to draw in mundane tourists, and that would likely be the beginning of the end for Haven Hollow. Could they even shut down a Hollow? I wasn't sure, but I also really didn't want to find out.

My hands were shaking so badly, it took me three tries to actually hit the buttons on my phone. But once I could, I started firing off emergency messages to the other council members. As soon as the messages were sent, I tried to come up with something to get the crowd to move on and stop taking pictures and videos of the gold tree.

The air was getting swimmy, and I wondered if I was having a panic attack for a brief second, because that would just be the absolute topper to this morning: to pass out in the middle of Main Street. But no, it wasn't that. The power that lay coiled up inside my rib cage like a sleeping dragon was getting agitated with my stress. I could feel it moving, sliding around, like it was looking for a way out of the cage it was confined to.

I froze, suddenly terrified. I was a potion maker. That was my thing, my family's thing, and it always had been. I didn't have big scary magic powers, and really, I had no idea what to do with the magic that I could feel waking up in my bones. Witch magic.

The faster I breathed, the stronger the power pulsed. It was a horrible cycle, my anxiety driving the magic, ratcheting it up, which made my panic spike even higher until I was stuck in a terrible feedback loop.

I clamped down as hard as I could on my own anxiety, but the magic surged even higher, fighting against me. Suddenly, a few bright sparks exploded nearby, and a couple people cried out as their phones shorted with a buzz of electricity. In response, they dropped them to the ground in little piles of broken plastic and scorched metal.

The *whoop whoop* of a police siren probably shouldn't have been as comforting as it was, but it let me breathe again as Taliyah inched her car down the road, occasionally giving another blare of her siren when people didn't clear out of her path fast enough.

She parked her cruiser at the side of the road, blocking the gold tree, and climbed out. With her hands planted on her hips and sweeping the edges of her suit jacket back (to make sure her badge was on full display), she turned to address the crowd.

"Okay, everyone. You all need to move

along—you're causing a major traffic block. And no more vandalizing the tree." She paused and faced the people directly in front of her. "Go on—get a move on. Yep, that means you, sir." Then she faced the crowd once more. "Let's get going! Now! Unless you want to spend the rest of your day behind bars!"

The last part was very pointed, and the crowd, which had started looking a bit guilty when she'd brought up the word 'vandalize' moved off quickly once it was clear no one was getting any more gold from the tree.

Once the crowd was gone, Taliyah glanced over, met my eyes, and beckoned me over.

"You want to tell me what's going on," she said in a hard tone that was very much Police Chief Morgan, and not Princess Olwen.

I shrugged helplessly. "You know as much as I do."

"How did you end up out here?" she asked, clearly taking issue with my statement.

I nodded and took a deep breath. "A customer came into my store, trying to barter with gold leaves, and she told me about a solid gold tree she'd seen just up the road. I came out here and started texting the council when it was obvious the woman wasn't just making it up."

Taliyah pinched the bridge of her nose, like she was trying to stave off a headache. "Okay.

I'm going to cordon the tree off and I'll get some officers up here to keep everyone away." She then called for backup.

"And what are we supposed to tell everyone who's already seen the tree?"

She shrugged. "That it was a stunt—something the town did for Halloween or something. I don't know—we'll come up with something. But for now, you get on the phone and get someone down here that can actually do something about this with magic."

Magic meant the coven, which meant Wanda. I winced. "I'm not sure how willing Wanda will be to help. She was pretty miffed about the accusations at the meeting."

Taliyah gave me a hard look. "Miffed enough to turn a tree into gold?"

Now, Wanda could be petty, I was the first to admit that. She'd grown up in a on old-school coven, where backstabbing, scheming, and petty vendettas were not only normal, but expected. But she took her role as High Witch of Scapegrace seriously, and she would never put her coven in danger by drawing attention to Haven Hollow. Never.

I shook my head, hard enough to make some of my hair slide free from the ponytail I'd put it in that morning. "No way. And it might be better if you don't ask those kinds of questions if you want her help because she can hold a grudge like no one can."

Taliyah's nostrils flared, but she gave a short, sharp nod. "Just get her here. I want this thing gone, yesterday."

It still wasn't quite noon, which meant there was absolutely no way that Wanda was up and about. So, that meant I got the fantastic job of waking up an irritated witch, in order to ask her a favor for the council that was currently on her shit list. Yes, I could actually swear when the occasion called for it. And this one definitely did. In fact: shit shit shit. And an added crap on top.

The longer the phone rang, the more anxious I got. What if Wanda was too deeply asleep to hear it ringing? Or what if she slept with her phone set to *do not disturb*, just so she wouldn't get woken up?

No, Wanda wouldn't do that. Not when someone in the coven might need her help. She'd complain about it, and make sure to let them know how terribly inconvenienced she was about the whole thing, but she'd never just ignore them.

The call went to voicemail, and with a little murmured apology, I hung up and hit redial. This time, the line picked up on the second ring, with an extremely groggy, "H'lo?"

"Wanda? It's Poppy. We have kind of a... well, we have a situation on Main Street. We could really, really use the powers of a High Witch, because... well, because it's quite the shitshow."

"If you're swearing, then it must be bad."

"It is. Really bad."

There were a few seconds of silence, and I worried that she'd fallen back asleep. "Wanda? Are you there?"

"Give me a minute, for spell's sake." I heard sheets rustling and a muffled yawn. "Do you have any idea what time it is?"

"Yes, and I'm sorry."

"Seriously, what part of 'nocturnal' do people not understand?"

I winced, wrapping one arm around my stomach while I watched Taliyah break out the bright yellow crime scene tape to cordon off the golden tree. "I'm really sorry, Wanda, but like I said—it's kind of an emergency."

"So, who died?"

"Jeez! No one died!"

"Then how much of an emergency can it really be?"

"Well, not that sort of emergency, thank the Lord, but something else has been turned into gold."

"Hopefully Roy?"

"I will choose to ignore that."

"You have no sense of humor, I swear." A sigh. "Okay, what's been turned to gold?"

"A whole tree, and it's right in the middle of Main Street! There are people everywhere, Wanda, tourists were taking pictures of it, before Taliyah chased them off. I don't see how this hasn't gotten out."

"Well," she said after a pause, sounding completely and totally uninterested. "You've got to give whoever is doing this some credit."

"Credit?"

"Sure. It's a pretty funny prank, if you ask me."

"Don't tell Taliyah that."

"I have no interest in being turned into a Wanda icicle, so you can bet your cheery, little gypsy butt that I won't."

"And... just a word of advice, maybe don't mention the fact that you were hoping it was Roy who was turned into gold."

She sighed out, long and hard. "Anything else, Poppy? I swear, you're getting so demanding in your old age."

"My old age?!" I asked, taken aback.

"Just a joke, bestie, calm your panties." Wanda then muttered something rude under her breath. "If Taliyah is already there, why are you calling me? Shouldn't we just let Bigfoot and the Princess get it all sorted out?" Then she laughed. "Bigfoot and the Princess—that sounds like a naughty romance novel I should be reading."

I let out a slow breath as the magic inside me sloshed against the inside of my ribs. "Wanda, please. This isn't them asking. This isn't even the council asking. This is me, your best friend, and I'm asking for your help because I'm scared. I'm scared of what this kind of attention would mean for Haven Hollow and I know you are the only person powerful enough to stop it." Sometimes you had to appeal to someone's sense of vanity to get anywhere.

"Well, that's certainly true."

"Please?"

"That is dirty pool," she growled across the line. "It's downright manipulative, Poppy Morton, and I hope you know that."

"Pretty please?"

"They both know that I'd tell them to go whistle. So, they get you to call me, knowing I can't say 'no' when you get that pathetic sound to your voice. Really, the nerve."

A tiny smile curled my lips. "Pretty please with a cherry on top?"

"Ah, spell. I trained you too well," she said, grudgingly. "I still won't be able to make it until sunset. But at least that will give me time to get the rest of the coven together and gather whatever ingredients and implements we'll need."

"That's fine."

She yawned again, longer this time. "Go to my store. Maverick's working today. Tell him to splash some repelling potion around the tree, or hex it to make people avoid it until we can get there with a more permanent solution."

I was so relieved, tears prickled in the corner of my eyes, and I had to blink rapidly to keep them from spilling. "Thank you, Wanda."

"Don't thank me," she grumbled. "I'm just doing it so I can rub it in Roy's nose later."

The smile got a little bit wider. "Okay. Thank you, anyway. I'll see you soon."

I hung up and walked over to tell Taliyah the plan, before trotting back down the street to collect a surly Warlock.

Chapter Eight

In all the pacing and fretting and waiting and worrying I was doing, I almost jumped out of my skin when the phone in my hand buzzed with an incoming text.

Hey, Mom, it read. *Is it okay if I stay late at school to work on a project? And then if I go to Marty's after? He's got a new video game we wanted to play.*

I fired back a quick text telling Finn that was fine and told him to let me know if he needed a ride home. At least that was one worry off my chest while I waited around to deal with this tree situation.

It was close to agonizing, waiting for the sun to set. I knew why Wanda was pretending so hard to be a vampire, to keep the coven and everyone else safe from vampire retaliation, and frankly, something like the gold tree would be the perfect way to lure her out and trick her into revealing herself. And from what I understood, there was some vampire woman who had been lurking around Haven Hollow, trying to catch Wanda in the act. So it was now more important than ever before for Wanda to keep the ruse up. Sure, I understood all that, but it didn't make the waiting any easier.

At least Maverick had come through, casting a quick repulsion hex on the tree that would keep mundanes from noticing it, and it even made Taliyah not want to spend much time standing next to it. So, the two of them stood together off to one side of the street discussing something (no doubt the tree), and I probably could have gone over to join them, but the way they were standing, kind of tilted in towards each other, their conversation seemed like it might have been intimate. Or at least private. So, I kept up my vigil, pacing a rut into the sidewalk and trying not to chew my nails down to bloody stumps.

I debated texting Andre with the information, but he wasn't on the council and council members weren't allowed to alert anyone to Haven Hollow matters unless they, too, were on the council. That, and I didn't want to interrupt whatever he was doing—which was, no doubt, learning new Magician tricks or deciding what next to teach Finn. Yes, I knew he wouldn't be upset with me for interrupting him, but I also wanted to maintain my own independence. I didn't want to lose myself to our relationship like I had with all the other men I'd been with. I wanted this one to be different—I wanted to still be Poppy, rather than Poppy and Andre. Maybe that sounded strange, but it was a good enough explanation to myself that I bought it and didn't bother him.

What felt like a thousand years later, the sun finally slipped beneath the horizon, sinking Haven Hollow into twilight. The antique street lights came on, and I tried not to notice how prettily the gold tree reflected their glow.

Not long after the sun had set, the rest of the coven arrived. Lorcan and Wanda came with Hellcat, Wanda's familiar. In a second car, Imani, the coven's newest member from Louisiana, drove Betanya and Olga, and their familiars, the racoon Franz, and Willie-Ray, the skunk. Maverick was already there with Isis, his owl, and me. Though, I wasn't about to be of any help during the ritual casting, I figured maybe I could just provide moral support. And I could try to keep the fighting to a minimum, because I was pretty sure things would blow up as soon as Roy showed up. And, strangely, he hadn't yet. I could only wonder if Maverick had done something with his magic to keep Roy at the Half-Moon or maybe things were just so busy there that Roy hadn't had a chance to come out for this. I had a feeling it was more the former than the latter, but I didn't ask because what I didn't know couldn't be used against me.

The first thing Circle Scapegrace did when they arrived was to cast a spell that was a bit like Maverick's repulsion hex, but on a larger scale. It filled the street with silvery mist, and would make sure people avoided the area, and didn't pay any attention to why a crowd of people and animals were all hanging around a plucked bare gold tree.

The witches all converged on the tree, prodding at its branches, and feeling its surface, as if trying to find some trace of the magic responsible. Olga even rapped her knuckles against the trunk, and the dull knocking told us that, however it had happened, the tree was solid gold all the way through.

Roy and Fifi pulled up about two hours later (which put to bed my belief that Maverick had somehow magicked Roy to stay away). As soon as Roy saw the tree, he started pacing and steadily working himself up into a bigger and bigger temper. I was worried he was going to burst if things didn't get handled, and soon.

Hellcat paced a circle around the tree, giving it a perfunctory sniff. "I think we should take it back to the coven house. It would make an adequate scratching post for a cat of my caliber."

Wanda ignored him, like she usually did. It was actually Imani who broke the news to the little hellion.

"Take it back to the house?! There's no way! This thing's got to weigh a thousand pounds, at least! It would crush a car."

Hellcat's tail lashed irritably. "Why do we even keep the vampire around if he and the Sasquatch can't relocate a simple tree? Ridiculous."

"I'm about to relocate you with my boot," Wanda muttered, not quite under her breath.

Hellcat hissed at her. "And to think they thought you were the one to do such a working. As if a dunce of your ineptitude were capable of such a feat, you miserable harpy."

Wanda gave him a long look before turning her gaze back to Imani. "What do you think? I bet if I listed Hellcat on Petfinder and offered someone twenty bucks to take him off my hands, they might?"

Imani hid her smile with her hand as Hellcat screeched in outrage.

"Can we get things rolling, here?" Roy cut

in. His jaw was clenched so tightly that I was shocked he'd gotten the words out without cracking a tooth.

Wanda just rolled her eyes and turned her back on him. "Alright, everyone. Take your positions."

Then Wanda faced me. Since I didn't have any witch magic, or at least, I wasn't *supposed* to have any witch magic, I wasn't expected to join in on the ritual. I figured I was more like the cheerleaders to the football team than an actual player. Rah-Rah, go Scapegrace!

"I need you to act as lookout," Wanda whispered to me.

I frowned. "Lookout for what?"

"A frumpy looking vampire woman who's trying to prove I'm not the vampire I'm trying to prove I am."

"Ah," I answered with a quick nod. "I haven't seen anyone who matches that description."

"Well, stay vigilant, would you?"

I nodded and took stock of our surroundings, not seeing anyone who wasn't supposed to be there. I watched as Wanda returned to her circle of witches and one Blood Warlock and they all took up position around the tree, linking their hands into a circle.

Honestly, once they got started, it didn't

take very long. There was some chanting, and the air got wavey, like a heat mirage over black asphalt. And after a few minutes, Wanda spoke a few commanding words, and hard metal gave way to sturdy dark wood. The metallic gold just bled away, like the wood was growing back over the top of it. Finally, the coven stepped back, shaking their hands out. Franz grabbed at Olga's skirts with his odd little hand-paws, and she scooped him up to ride on her shoulder. The lederhosen he was wearing made him look like Rocket Raccoon from The Avengers dressed as a German for Halloween.

"Crisis averted." Wanda tossed her long dark hair back over her shoulder with a practiced sweep of her arm. Then she braced one hand on her hip and pointed at the ground in front of her while glaring at the people assembled. "The line for apologies starts here, by the way. And, Roy, you can be first."

Roy crossed his arms over his chest, scowling. The move made his biceps swell until they looked bigger than my head—not that I noticed. I was perfectly happy with my Mr. Darcy.

"Is that seriously what you're worried about right now, Wanda?" he demanded. "We have way bigger problems. If it wasn't your coven who did this, then it seems like a very deliberate attack."

"*If* it wasn't my coven?" she repeated, suddenly fuming.

"No one thinks it was your coven," Taliyah interrupted, spearing a glance at Roy. "Do we?"

He grumbled something but then begrudgingly agreed with a quick nod.

"Attack?" I repeated, reminded of his previous comment. That sounded serious. I tugged at the sleeves of my sweater, twisting the fabric. "Why do you think that?"

Roy waved a massive hand at the once more wooden tree. "Something this big and flashy? Right in the heart of downtown, which gets the most traffic? It had to be deliberate. Either someone was screwing around and their screwing around got out of hand, or they did this on purpose to bring a lot of unwanted attention to Haven Hollow. Either way, this is dangerous to us, especially with things as precarious as they are now." He took a breath. "And, again, I'm left to wonder who has this sort of power to begin with. And I keep only returning to—"

"The coven," Maverick answered for him, eyes narrowed. "What makes you so sure it was one of us?" Isis clicked her beak in irritation. "Poppy admitted that one of her potions had this kind of effect. It could have been her. Or anyone who got their hands on her potion," he amended when Imani jabbed him in the ribs with an elbow.

I bit my lip and twisted my sleeve harder. "I mean, *Gypsy Gold* couldn't do this. Like I said before, it turns things into *Fool's* gold, and only for an hour or so. I've never seen anything like *this*."

"Maverick has a point, though," Taliyah said, her eyes narrowed in thought. "What about your son? He's a teenager, right? And he has his own magic?"

"Finn wouldn't do this. And he's a Magician, not a brewer of potions."

Taliyah didn't look convinced. "Maybe this is his version of a bit of youthful rebellion?"

My magic roiled angrily, and I did my best to stuff it back down. It was instinctual to get defensive of someone accusing my son of such a horrible thing.

"No," Wanda said, shaking her head. "Finn isn't like that. He's a good kid."

I gave her a nod of thanks. Yes, sometimes Finn struggled. But everyone did at his age. Growing up was hard, and heck, I still struggled and I hadn't been a teenager for many long years. Though, I had to admit to myself that Finn did seem to be struggling more lately. He was quiet, and obviously troubled by something. The thought made my heart feel too tight, like it was stuck in a jar and couldn't beat properly.

"Finn wouldn't do this," I repeated, my lips stiff. "Besides, he couldn't have done it. I only made one vial of the potion, like I said, and Andre took it with him when he left to go to Portland."

"Andre? The new Magician in town?" Taliyah asked.

"Yes, and..." I cleared my throat. "My boyfriend."

"Could he have done this?" Taliyah asked, apparently missing the part where I said Andre was my boyfriend.

I frowned. "He wasn't even in town when the bush was turned to gold."

"Are you sure?" Roy asked bluntly. "I mean, how much do you really know about this guy? He just shows up one day out of nowhere, and ends up moving into a house right up the street from you? Do you even know where he's from? Do you really know anything about him?"

The absolute unfairness of that comment, especially coming from Roy, had my words getting all jammed up in the back of my mouth. It wasn't like I'd gone around announcing my relationship with Andre, but Roy had his own soulmate. He should have known what it was like to find the one and I was sure Fifi had told him about Andre's and my connection because

I'd talked about it with the girls at the Black Cat Cocktail Club.

"I'm going to choose not to take offense to that," I managed, proud of myself that I was keeping my anger in check. "And I would ask you, for the sake of playing devil's advocate, even if Andre were behind this, what would even be the point? To turn a tree gold? To put Haven Hollow at risk? Why would he want to do that?"

"Wow," Wanda cut in dryly before I could find my voice again. She was facing Roy, and she was fuming mad. I could tell by the way she held her shoulders. "I thought your only power was showing up in blurry photographs, Roy, but apparently it's your ability to leap to huge conclusions with a single bound and not a shred of evidence."

Roy turned on her, glaring from beneath heavy brows. "I don't see you trying to figure anything out. Maybe you should care more about protecting the town than about your own pride."

Wanda gave him an astonished look. "Why in the name of the Goddess would I do that when my pride is the most important thing to me?" she demanded, clearly mocking him. "Besides, I just fixed the problem." She motioned to the once golden tree. "You're welcome, by the way, you ungrateful ape."

"You've fixed the problem for now." Roy ran a hand back through his hair. "What about the next time this happens?"

Wanda waved a dismissive hand. "It could have been a fluke that won't happen again."

"Once is an accident, twice is a pattern," Roy answered, turning to face everyone else. "We need to figure out why this is happening, and we need to stop it."

Roy took a step forward, and Lorcan was suddenly standing beside Wanda, his lip peeled back to reveal the sharp edges of his fangs. I hadn't even seen him arrive.

"We can't just assume everything is fine," Roy growled. "Do you not grasp how badly this could go for the town?"

"Do you not understand that flinging random accusations at people and causing this kind of a rift in the council could be bad for this town?" Wanda snapped back.

Then Fifi was pushing between them. Well, she put her back to Roy's chest and shoved him back a step, anyway. "Okay, time out. No more fighting. This is not what we need right now. We need to be sticking together and trusting in one another to get to the bottom of this."

Roy stopped like he'd been stuck in play, looking down at Fifi, his chest rising and falling rapidly. She patted him absently, but looked at Wanda and then everyone else. "Clearly, we need to talk about this. But is the middle of the road the best spot for a conversation? The spell won't last forever. How about we hold an emergency council session at the Half-Moon, and try to hash this out?" Fifi then gave a pointed look to Roy and Wanda. "Hash it out peacefully."

"Fine," Roy grumbled, and turned to stalk up the street, pausing only long enough for Fifi to catch up with him.

Taliyah got back into her cruiser after a quick word with Maverick, and went to move it somewhere a little more inconspicuous, like an actual parking spot.

Wanda rolled her eyes and turned to the rest of the coven. "This is going to be annoying. Good work tonight, everyone, but don't bother waiting up. Imani," she continued. "Would you take Hellcat with you? It's going to be aggravating enough without his scathing diatribes. Just stuff him in the trunk if he acts up."

Ignoring Hellcat's offended yowl, she turned to saunter up the street towards the bar, holding Lorcan's hand.

I shot a text to Finn to make sure he'd gotten to Marty's okay, and when I got a thumbs up in response, I pulled my cardigan a little tighter around myself and headed up the street.

Chapter Nine

While Hallowed Homes was certainly a nice spot for a meeting, with comfortable chairs and really good coffee, there was food at the Half-Moon so, in my mind, it had Hallowed Homes beat.

Roy closed the place up early, citing a plumbing issue for the mundane customers, so we had the place to ourselves, and we could sprawl out at the comfy booths and tables (which was good because I thought Wanda and Roy might come down to fists and magic).

There was a reason that the Half-Moon did such good business, and that wasn't all about its location. The place was warm, inviting, with its polished wood floors and the heavy oak bar on the back wall, where Roy could usually be found slinging drinks, since he seemed to struggle with keeping a bartender on.

But the food was the real draw. It was all pub style stuff, mostly burgers and hot sandwiches, but they did have some really tasty entrees and salads. And I'd always found that meetings went better when everyone wasn't hangry, especially after hours.

So, I didn't feel any guilt at all as I tucked into my cheeseburger and fries, even if I was going to have to walk a few extra miles to burn it all off again. It was exactly the right side of delicious and comforting, and I was going to take the extra helping of fries Roy had heaped on the side as an apology for earlier.

As I sat there, I got a text from Andre, asking how my day was.

Just in the middle of a council meeting, I texted back, feeling giddy even though I tried to stop myself. *What are you doing later?*

Hopefully coming to see you? he texted back.

I hope so, I responded with a happy face. *Text you once I'm out of here.*

He responded with a thumbs up and just in time for Taliyah, who hadn't asked for anything but a ginger ale with lots of ice, to tap her knuckles against the table once everyone was settled.

"The tree and the bush aren't actually the only gold related problems we're having in Haven Hollow," she explained grimly. "The reason I happened to be close by this morning was because there was a robbery of a jewelry store over on first street that was reported right before this tree business came up. And it wasn't your run of the mill robbery either."

"Of course not," Maverick grumbled. "Because that would be too easy."

She nodded at him. I did notice that Angelo wasn't present and hadn't been all day. Apparently, he was taking this bodyguarding business of Lydia pretty seriously—something which still surprised me. But, who knew, maybe even the biggest womanizers could change their ways with the right woman. Or maybe Lydia was simply his newest flavor craze. Whatever the answer, it really wasn't my business.

"Whoever robbed the place," Taliyah continued. "Didn't set off a single alarm, and they made off with every scrap of gold in the building, leaving behind everything else."

"Wait." Fifi looked up from her root beer float, confused. "They took *only* the gold?"

Taliyah nodded, like Fifi had just asked a really good question. "Exactly. They left all the other precious and semi-precious metals, taking only the gold."

"Then they left—" I started.

"—silver bracelets, necklaces, rings. And platinum versions of the same—as well as some pretty expensive gemstones. All left behind. In one instance, they pried a sapphire from its setting to take the gold necklace, but left the stone." Then Taliyah breathed out a big breath. "Which makes zero sense."

Wanda frowned, probably still miffed that Roy had ignored her request for a glass of red wine. "So, the thieves are good enough at what they do to break in without getting caught, but stupid enough to leave some of the most valuable pieces behind?"

Taliyah shrugged. "I'm just bringing it up because it was odd and gold related. It may or may not be linked to our not so merry gilder."

Roy sat next to Fifi, holding her hand, but still glowering. "I keep coming back to Poppy's potion."

"Of course," I grumbled, shaking my head.

He nodded. "I'm sorry, Poppy, but it's just too big a coincidence."

I finished chewing my bite of cheeseburger before I answered. "I know. That's why I brought it up in the first place. I'm just not sure how my potion fits into any of this. Like I said, it makes Fool's gold, light and pretty, but not valuable. And I only made one vial, and I know

Andre used it, because he sent me pictures of the things he turned into Fool's gold. And, no, no one could have copied the potion because no one was with me when I brewed it. And, before you bring it up again, no, Finn had nothing to do with it." I took a breath. Something else was nagging at me. "Here's the problem." I gestured from myself, to Taliyah, to Roy and Wanda. "Let's assume that all the gold related events are related to each other. If someone did steal my potion, and they somehow altered it so that it made *real* gold instead of fake, then why on earth would they need to *steal* gold from a jewelry store? Why not just make the gold themselves? It just doesn't make any sense."

Everything was quiet for a minute while we all mulled that over.

It was Fifi who broke the silence, playing with the straw from her float. "Maybe we need to look at the people who are new to town? We haven't really been able to vet people like we used to. I'm not saying we should go back to Ophelia's way of doing things," she added in a hurry. "But maybe someone slipped in who has a grudge against the Hollow and now they're taking that grudge out on us and we just didn't look at their backgrounds closely enough?"

"Have there been any people new in town with..." Taliyah made a face, gesturing vaguely. “Gold powers, lately?” There was a tinge of faint pink in her cheeks, like she was embarrassed by the question, and she picked up her ginger ale to take a drink to hide it.

“The only new people I know of are Lydia, Poppy’s cousin, and Andre, Poppy’s boyfriend,” Roy said. “And Lydia has been under strict watch by Angelo since he seems to believe she’s in some kind of trouble. So that just leaves Andre.”

“Who had nothing to do with this,” I answered, giving him a look.

“Fifi, who else is new to town?” Wanda asked as she then faced Roy. “Because Mr. Darcy I’m sure had nothing to do with this.”

“Mr. Darcy?” Roy repeated, frowning.

Wanda waved an unconcerned hand at him. “It’s a character from a classic book—but, since you can’t read, you wouldn’t know it.”

“Wanda, please,” Taliyah said, frowning at the witch who got an expression of ‘who, me?’ on her face.

Fifi nibbled on her lip as she thought about Wanda’s question, clearly deciding to ignore her later commentary, which was just as well. “There was a leprechaun, I think. But they’re more about hiding gold than making it.”

“Any dragons?” Lorcan asked, teasing.

Fifi didn’t seem to get the joke. “No, still

just Gregor," she answered, talking about one of her surlier realtors at the office. "And again, he's more about hoarding gold than making it and showing it off in very public places."

"A dragon wouldn't have left the tree in the ground," Wanda grumbled. "They would have made off with it."

"Right," Fifi said as she started toying with her napkin, twisting it between her fingers. "No one really springs to mind. Maybe we could go over the applications of those who recently moved here again and see if anyone or anything jumps out?"

Roy patted her hand. "It's a good plan. We'll do that."

"We do need to do something." I bit my lip, still trying to put all the pieces together.

The problem was, a lot of dangerous and violent things had happened in Haven Hollow over the past few years. Roy was right about one thing, though; something as big and flashy and obviously weird as bushes and trees turning to gold was only going to draw the wrong kind of attention, which the town could not handle at the moment.

"Alright," Taliyah said, looking tired. She tossed back the rest of her drink. "It's as good a plan as any. If anything else happens, I'll let you all know. No point in trying to figure this out until we have a chance to get some more information."

So, everyone finished up and headed off with a tentative action plan. I was still hoping that Wanda was right, that it was all a fluke or a dumb prank, and things would get back to normal, and I could stop feeling vaguely guilty about something that had nothing to do with me. At least, I was pretty sure it had nothing to do with me.

And, yes, I could have brought up the fact that my magic was off lately—that there was a chance I'd somehow unknowingly turned the bush and tree to gold by creating the *Gypsy Gold* potion, even if I hadn't actually used it. But I felt that was a conversation I needed to have with Wanda first, before I announced it to everyone else. Because maybe it wasn't such a big deal—maybe my magic taking on the feel of the coven's—maybe that was just part and parcel of being in a coven? I wasn't sure, but I really didn't want to deal with more of Roy's suspicion that would certainly ensue if I brought any of this up. So, I didn't.

I got home just before Marty dropped Finn off, and it did make me feel a bit better that, while Marty didn't get out of the car, he did wave when he saw me opening the door for Finn. He also gave a little light honk of his car horn before backing out of the driveway again.

Finn looked tired, but he was smiling when he dropped his book bag on the floor of the living room.

"Still full of hot dogs, or are you hungry?" I teased him, smoothing his hair back off his forehead.

Finn blinked, his grin coming just a second too late. "Yep. Me and Marty really pigged out. I'm going to head to bed. Goodnight, Mom."

And he was heading upstairs before I could even respond.

"Oh, okay. Goodnight," I told his feet before they disappeared off the stairs.

The feeling of something not being right only got stronger. But I'd asked Finn too many times already if something was going on with him and each time he said he was fine. So I figured he'd tell me when he was ready to or he'd figure it out himself. Either way, it was clear he didn't want to involve me so I wouldn't force the issue.

Just then, Andre texted me to see if I still wanted to get together but I suddenly didn't feel like it was such a good idea. Not with Finn acting so out of sorts. And if there was a chance my son might feel like opening up to me, I wanted to make sure it was just the two of us, in case he didn't want an audience. So, I told Andre I wasn't feeling up to it and he responded good-naturedly just like I knew he would.

It was a restless night, just as I'd known it would be.

The next morning, I went into work early, and upon looking up the road as I parked in front of my store, my heart sank when I noticed the gold tree was no longer wood, but was once again gleaming gold in the sun.

I sent off a text to the council group chat, and ten minutes after that, Roy came screeching up in his truck.

It took him two tries, but eventually, he managed to rip the whole tree right out of the ground.

***

The council group chat had been buzzing all morning, with questions and arguments and accusations flying so fast, it was hard for me to even keep up.

No one could figure out why the tree had turned back to gold. Roy was accusing Wanda of doing the ritual incorrectly on purpose. Wanda said she was seconds away from turning Roy into a real ape, among other less savory things. Taliyah, Fifi and I were trying to determine if the tree was turned back to gold on purpose, or if it had simply changed on its own. The bigger question was: how would you even test that kind of thing?

With the tree now stashed in the Half-Moon's storage room for the moment, at least the issue wasn't a pressing one. Still, it was just one more mystery on top of the pile of unsolved mysteries this town had become, and we hadn't even started to crack the other ones.

The only respite in the stream of angry text messages occurred when Henner popped into the chat.

I've done what I can to scrub all the photos and videos from the internet of the gold tree, he typed. *But I can't do much about any images people still have on their phones, unless they connect to local WIFI. And don't even get me started if someone had an actual film camera.*

I relaxed a little bit. That was one worry taken care of, at least. Henner might not think of his own magic as impressive compared to his grandmother Betanya's, but the things he could do technology-wise were just incredible.

Another message then popped up from Henner.

And, of course, there isn't much I can do about people who saw the tree in person. I'll keep an eye on any message boards or social media, but gossip will probably still spread.

He was right, of course. Word of mouth was still a thing. Hopefully, without any hard evidence, people would think it was just a stunt or a prank, and maybe even start to doubt their own memories. I mean, in the grand scheme of things, how crazy was a gold tree, really?

And there was also no way for Henner to know how many people had seen the pictures and videos before he'd taken care of them on the net. We needed everything in Haven Hollow to be nice and calm for a while in order to allow things to blow over. At least before the next crisis hit.

I bit my lip and slid my phone back into my pocket. There wasn't anything I could do about that situation, and I still had customers in the store that needed attention.

I spent a few hours bustling about, tidying the shelves and making notes about which potions needed restocking. It was busy enough for me not to have time to dwell on things too much, as I helped people pick out exactly what they were looking for: whether that was a potion for a peaceful night's sleep, or something to put a little more pep in their step, or something to help their memory, or a love potion.

I'd just carefully wrapped up a purchase from the last customer when the bell clanging over the door alerted me to the fact that two more women had just entered the shop. Judging from their appearance, I would have imagined they were in their late forties, probably. They were both dressed in sweatshirts and jeans under light jackets, clearly out for a day of shopping. But with the way they were shaking their heads and speaking in low tones to one another, I couldn't help but wonder if something was up. I couldn't hear what they were saying until they made their way a little further into the shop.

"I'd heard this was a safe little town," the first woman, the one wearing chunky bracelets to match her necklace, said. "But now I'm not so sure."

"I know what you mean. It's scary." Her friend, the one with sunglasses on top of her head, pursed her lips. "Honestly, I'm wondering if we should just head home a bit early. I just don't feel good about this anymore. It was so close to the hotel."

Well, that didn't sound good. I spoke up when they were a bit closer to the counter. "Hello, ladies. I'm sorry, I didn't mean to eavesdrop on your conversation, but is everything okay? Do either of you need help?"

I never wanted anyone to feel unsafe in Haven Hollow, not the people who made their homes here, and not the people who visited.

Chunky bracelets turned to me. "Oh, we're

just fine. We were just talking about what happened at the antique store a few roads over. It's just awful."

I knew the store they were talking about—Timeless Treasures. In fact, I'd been in there a few times myself. They always had fun things. I'd even picked up a few of my brass display candle holders there. The man who ran the place, Mr. Wells, was human, and very nice.

"No, why, did something happen? Is the owner okay?"

"You didn't hear about what happened?" Chunky bracelets asked.

"The owner looked alright, just a bit upset, and I can't really blame him." Sunglasses shook her head.

"The place was robbed in the night. It's crawling with police right now," Bracelets responded.

"Oh, that's awful." And, of course, it brought to mind the robbery of the jewelry store that Taliyah had mentioned. "Do you know if the thieves made off with much?"

Losing any stock would be terrible, of course, but there were some pieces that were truly irreplicable. Mr. Wells hunted down his inventory all on his own, going to estate sales and auctions. He had so many stories about his 'treasure hunts', as he called them.

"Well." Chunky bracelet's eyes darted from one side of the store to the other. "We weren't listening in on purpose, of course. But from what the police were saying, whoever broke in left some of the more expensive or rare pieces behind, and only took the gold."

I wasn't surprised to hear that.

Sunglasses snorted, rolling her eyes. "Can you imagine? They're not just thieves, they're snobs. Grabbing up any scrap of gold, but leaving the glassware and the hundred-year-old platinum engagement ring behind."

Chunky bracelets leaned forward, like she was telling a scandalous secret. "They even took an old gold tooth. A tooth! Who would want something like that?"

"That's so weird," I said, my voice thin. I hoped they couldn't see the way my hands were twisting into fists behind the counter.

Gold stolen from the antique store? Right after the jewelry store, and the tree up the road turning to gold? Twice now? And the bush. This couldn't be a coincidence, and it didn't mean anything good for the town. The chances of this being a prank or something random were fading rapidly by the second.

My lips were bloodless, and a little numb, but I forced them into a customer service smile. "That is awful. I promise you; Haven Hollow really is a safe place. That kind of thing usually never happens here, but it must have been very shocking for you. I hope it doesn't damage your opinion of the town."

"Well." Chunky bracelets darted a look between her friend and me. "It has been very nice so far."

Sunglasses nodded grudgingly.

"Feel free to look around. If you need any help, please let me know." *Just smile, be polite, and wait for them to move on,* I told myself.

When they were busy looking through the shelves towards the back of the store, I got my phone out again.

I had a sinking suspicion about all the missing gold. I couldn't be sure I was right, since I didn't know much about magic other than potion making, but it was worth mentioning.

So, I shot a text to the council group chat, asking if everyone could meet at the Half-Moon for lunch.

Wanda couldn't leave the house, but there were work arounds for that.

In the meantime, I just had to sit back, smile, and pretend like everything was just fine.

I was getting uncomfortably good at that.

Chapter Ten

The work around was that Fifi called Wanda and Wanda was able to FaceTime into the meeting.

By the time I managed to get to the bar, the rest of the council was already there. Or, as there as they physically could be, at least. Roy had set us up in one of the more private areas, one that was usually reserved for birthday parties and private dinners. It meant we could spread out and paw through some of the applications the council had received over the last year without having to worry about someone at the next table seeing or hearing too much. We already had enough problems on our hands, we didn't need to add to them by being careless.

When I walked up to the table, everyone

was elbow deep in papers already, with a few glasses of water scattered between them.

Taliyah held one sheet up, squinting at it. "What about this guy, Leif Olagson? He's a smith, and a… *svartalflar*? Am I even saying that right?" Then she shook her head, her expression one of '*how did that sentence even come out of my mouth?*'

"Yes," Roy grumbled, distracted by his own pile. "They're dark elves, from Scandinavia. But they just work gold, they don't make it, or even mine it."

"Ugh." Taliyah sighed and dropped the application back to the table. "I remember the days where all I had to worry about were *normal* crimes committed by *normal* people. I never thought I'd actually miss a straight up assault charge, but here we are."

"Oh!" Fifi sat up, excited. "What about this one? Francesco Almirante, he's an alchemist! And don't alchemists turn things into gold?"

On the screen of Fifi's phone, Wanda waved a dismissive hand. "No, sorry. I've met Francesco and it can't be him."

"Why not?" Roy growled.

"Well, for one, he's retired, and the only thing he ever managed to change was gold into lead. Not many people were interested in that, as you can imagine. There's a reason he's looking to live in a Hollow."

Fifi sagged back into the booth's soft bench. "Darn."

"Maybe *you* should come up with some suggestions, Wanda," Roy said tightly. The paper in his hands crinkled with the force of his grip.

Wanda took an obnoxious slurp of her coffee, loud enough that it could literally be heard across town and through the speakers on Fifi's phone. "Buddy, this is the middle of the night for me. You're lucky I'm participating at all."

A muscle ticked in Roy's jaw, and I saw him pulling in a deep breath, probably to say something that would make the situation even worse, so I tried to jump in.

"Um, hi everyone. Hi, Wanda," I waved to her, and she muttered something into her cup. "I didn't mean to drag everyone away from your busy lives." I scooted down the bench, a little closer to where Taliyah was sitting, so I could see Wanda easier. "Taliyah, I heard about the antique store robbery. Are there any suspects?" I had a hunch, but whether or not that hunch panned out would depend on her answer.

Taliyah clenched her jaw, looking irritated. "No one. No one saw anything, no alarms were tripped. The owner even had security cameras in the place, but did they pick up anything? Of course not, because that would have been just too damned easy. One second the gold items were there, the next, gone."

A little frisson of nervous excitement rolled through my belly like bubbles in soda. This information made my theory even more likely.

"The cameras didn't get *anything*?" Fifi shook her head, stunned.

"Not a damn thing." Taliyah tossed back the rest of her water like she wished it was something stronger. "Not even a shadow. The cameras must have been tampered with, but I can't tell how. That or we're dealing with an invisible species."

Roy frowned, tapping his finger against the table. "Maybe ask Henner to look into it? He might be able to spot what they did, if they did, in fact, tamper with the cameras."

"Or," I said, a flush rising up into my cheeks. I just hoped I wasn't about to say something really stupid. "What if no one took it?"

Taliyah looked at me, her expression too tired and fed-up to be angry. "You think it was an inside job?"

"What? No! Mr. Wells would never. No, sorry. Let me start over." I took a deep breath. "I think you're right, Taliyah, about all the cases being connected."

Everyone was now paying attention. Even Wanda looked interested, as far as I could tell, with half of her face hidden by her coffee cup.

"Explain," Roy said.

"Okay, hear me out." I took a deep breath and nodded. "What if someone is turning things in town into gold, but in doing so, is *draining* gold from nearby stores?" I glanced around, but no one was scowling or telling me that was a dumb idea, so I continued. "That was why no one was seen stealing the gold from the jewelry store the night the tree turned to gold. Or the antique store, on the night the tree turned back into gold. And remember all those items going missing before either break-in? I think you said something about household jewelry and dishes going missing?"

Taliyah nodded. "Right."

"Maybe those all either were gold or had gold in them," I continued. "The point I'm trying to make is that whatever power or spell we're dealing with... well, what if it just kind of absorbed whatever gold was in the vicinity?"

There was a moment of silence as everyone looked at each other. No one was pointing or laughing at me, either, so it couldn't have been too bad an idea.

Wanda actually put her coffee down. "That's actually entirely possible," she said, slowly. "But I've never heard of a spell that could do such a thing. It would explain why the change of objects to gold is permanent, though."

Roy rubbed his eyes and then scraped his hand over his face. His stubble was coming in thick, and I could hear the rasp of it against his palm even across the table. "But then we're back to the same question; who would be capable of magic like that?"

No one had an answer for that one.

My phone beeped then, followed by everyone else's at the table, including Wanda's from the sound of it. My stomach sank. That wasn't a good sign.

I opened up the council chat to find a message from Henner that read; *You're not going to like this*. And then a video clip beneath it.

It was Roy who ended up hitting play on the clip, his face in grim lines. We all crowded a little closer to watch.

The screen was filled with the face of a pretty young woman, in her early twenties probably. Her blonde hair was pulled back by a black scarf that had little cartoon ghosts on it. She grinned at the camera as the video started playing.

"Hey fam," she chirped, her head tipping to one side. "This is me, Kenzie Chase, here with *Chasing the Paranormal*. I've gotten your DMs, and I wanted you to know that I'm here, in Haven Hollow, to give you exactly what you're asking for."

The scene then shifted to a location with more shade, the shadows falling over Kenzie's face. "Yep, you heard right. I'm here in Haven Hollow, Oregon, following the story of a town where random objects have begun to turn to gold. Is this a paranormal event, or just a hoax the locals have put on for the tourists? Either way, we're in for a trip, right? So, join me, while I get to the bottom of what's going on in this supposedly sleepy little town. Could Haven Hollow be a hotbed of paranormal events? You can soon decide for yourself."

The camera zoomed out, showing Kenzie standing in front of the Haven Hollow sign that welcomed people into town, with Kenzie framed right in the middle, and '*Chasing the Paranormal*' scrawled across the top.

No one said anything.

Instead, we all sat there in horrified silence for a long moment. Then Roy swore so viciously that I was surprised it didn't peel the varnish right off the wooden table. His phone creaked in protest as his hand clenched around it.

Wanda stared down into her coffee mug, like she was thinking of adding a splash of something stronger, and I couldn't blame her.

“What are we going to do?” Fifi asked in a tight whisper.

“Well, look on the bright side,” Wanda said, a humorless smile on her face. “Maybe we’ll get lucky, and she’ll end up turning into gold.”

***

Kenzie Chase descended on Haven Hollow like one of the biblical plagues, but somehow more annoying.

It seemed every time someone turned around, there she was, poking her nose and her camera lens into everything. The council group chat was lighting up with sightings of her: at the cemetery, the woods, some of the older and closed, even condemned buildings. I’d even seen her myself, poking around at the spot where the gold tree had been, before Roy had relocated it.

The girl was a menace.

But what could we do? She wasn’t doing anything wrong, other than occasional trespassing, but Taliyah could only give her a warning —not arrest her. And we couldn’t exactly boot her out of the town, especially without making her even more suspicious than she already was. Sure, we could drum up some spells that might make her want to avoid certain locations, but those spells weren't permanent. And as soon as she returned to her hotel, she'd no doubt make note to herself to investigate said locations again.

And if Wanda performed a spell to wipe her memory, all it would take was one of her fans reminding her of her newest investigation into Haven Hollow and I was sure she'd return, probably even more determined. No, using magic in this case was going to be too dangerous.

Henner had been doing his best to make sure any videos Kenzie took ended up corrupted and unusable as soon as she attempted to upload them to the web, but that just seemed to make her more determined.

I was rushing around the kitchen, throwing things together in Finn's lunch bag early one morning, trying to get us both out the door in time, when I got a notification on my phone that there had been an update on Kenzie's channel.

Caught somewhere between fear that she'd actually found something worth mentioning, and hope that she was finally giving up and leaving town, I opened the video.

In it, Kenzie was standing just outside of Stomper's Creamery, using the striped red and white awning to frame her. She was smiling, but there was something about her eyes that made me nervous.

"Hey, fam," she chirped to the camera. "I haven't been making much headway in this case, as people are surprisingly quiet and don't seem to want to talk to me. I'm not giving up, but there might be more going on in this town than I thought."

Uh, oh. My stomach sank.

"You've probably noticed that I've been a bit sparse with my posting? Well, funny story about that. Yesterday, I wanted to document the place where some of the possible paranormal phenomena occurred, but the tree that turned to gold is now gone, of course. In fact, it looked like it was pulled right out of the ground, not even roots left behind." She raised her brows at that. "In fact," she lowered her voice then, and glanced around like she was worried about being overheard while making a video she was going to post online for hundreds of thousands of viewers. "The video ended up so corrupted, I couldn't even upload it. Weird, right? Truth is, most of my videos are ending up super messed up. They work on my camera when I watch them, but as soon as I attempt to upload them, they're destroyed. Coincidence much?"

She brought the camera up close to her face, and I could see irritation warring with excitement in her eyes. "It's probably just a matter of time before something happens to this one," she continued, as I immediately texted Henner to let him know he'd missed one. And an important one, at that. After I'd texted him, I returned to Kenzie's video.

"I think something is going on in Haven Hollow. Something big. And someone doesn't want me to find out just what that something is. But don't worry, fam. No way am I giving up. Keep checking my channel for updates and don't forget to heart and follow. See you on the spooky side."

I sighed and rubbed my forehead. This was beyond annoying. It was hard enough trying to figure out what was going on in town without some supernatural Nancy Drew sneaking around and spying on everyone. Not to mention, more and more objects were showing up turned to gold. I'd started driving a weird, zig-zag route to and from work, trying to spot any rocks, mailboxes, or anything else that might show up gilded. In one situation, I'd had to call Roy about a board sign that was now gleaming gold. The thing easily weighed over two hundred pounds, and there was just no way for me to lift it and stick it in my Jeep.

And I wasn't the only one. The council was going out of their way to scour the town, trying to keep ahead of the gold plague, before a pesky ghost hunter could catch sight of them. But we still couldn't figure out what was causing it all. Or why. Or how to stop it.

And the pattern of things turning to gold... well, it wasn't happening in a pattern at all! It was more like someone had been walking through town, spying this and that and then zapping those things with a gold-making gun.

It did seem like there was some weight to my theory about how the spell worked, because Taliyah mentioned that the police station was being flooded with reports of thefts from all over town. Haven Hollow residents were finding gold items stolen from their homes in more and more bizarre ways.

Jewelry. Fillings. Candle holders. One baffled woman reported that the gold inlay at the edges of her mother's fancy China had vanished overnight. And how in the world was that possible? It was getting more difficult to explain it all as one burglar. And we weren't getting any closer to finding out who was doing it, or how.

Everyone was stressed and snapping at each other, and with all the difficulties that Haven Hollow had faced over the past few years, the threat of being exposed by such a bizarre bit of magic was a stress no one needed.

I leaned back against the cabinets and stuffed my phone into my purse. I just couldn't bear to hear the ping of the group chat for one second longer. All the accusations and the sniping back and forth, it was twisting my stomach into knots.

I hated all the suspicion, and I hated what it was doing to us. Because doubts had started to worm their way into my head, I kept thinking back to that bottle of *Gypsy Gold* I'd made for Andre. It still seemed like it was too big a coincidence—that the moment I'd made the potion, suddenly we were under attack by a golden curse?

Ever since Alecto the Fury boiled into town, I'd been even more nervous about the idea of my own magic being out of control. She'd turned my own powers back on me like a curse, a fitting 'punishment' for breaking Marty's heart. Fortunately, Marty had defended me, and told the Fury right to her face that he didn't want me punished. And that had pretty much been the end of that.

But my magic had still ultimately been the source of my own misery, reaching out into every aspect of my life and turning my life against me: potions going wrong, accidents, misfortune and strife. So, I couldn't help but be a little paranoid about every roil and gurgle of power running through my bones.

Was I the one responsible for this gold business? Had my subconscious somehow done it? Had the potion, one I hadn't made in years, gone wrong and this new magic of mine had fueled it? But if that was the case, how was it happening? And why were some objects turning to gold randomly throughout the town—objects that seemingly had nothing to do with me?

The only other option was that someone close to me had taken the *Gypsy Gold* potion, and had somehow changed it and was now turning things to gold deliberately. But who would do such a thing?

I'd only made one potion, and Finn hadn't even touched the bottle. The only other option then was Andre. But even the thought of that hurt my heart.

I suddenly felt sick. As a Magician, I believed Andre had the power required to borrow the gold from one item in order to turn another object into gold. I mean, I wasn't sure about that, but Magicians possessed magic. It wasn't witch magic, true, but it was still magic.

Furthermore, Andre had had the potion in his possession, and he'd definitely been out of town. Hadn't he? I mean, he'd sent me pictures, but how could I be sure if those pictures were new? He could have taken them years ago—but why would he have taken shots of gold items? The other answer was—he could have forged them with his own magic. But the question still remained: why? Why in the world would he sneak back into town with a bunch of made-up stories about his travels, and fake images, while secretly turning random things to gold?

He wouldn't. No one would. It made absolutely no sense. But what else was I supposed to think? The accusations in the council group chat were getting wilder and wilder, and their paranoia was starting to get to me.

I didn't think Andre would do anything like that, and he certainly wouldn't lie about it—I mean, I didn't think he would, anyway. I knew him, in a way I'd never known anyone in my life. I knew him down to his soul—I knew him almost like I knew myself. But that was a soul connection. As to our own separate experiences and the stories that made us both us, I didn't know him as well. In fact, I didn't know him that well at all. But even so, our soul connection was such that I could feel the truth—and that truth told me there was no way he'd done this.

Andre took his job as a Magician seriously. He spent his life helping children, and inspiring hope in people, making the world a brighter place. Yes, there was no way he was responsible.

But what if I was wrong? My track record with men was hard to ignore.

The clock on the stove ticked over, and I yelped when I saw the time. If Finn and I didn't leave in the next two minutes, we were going to be late dropping him off at school.

"Finn," I called up the stairs. "Come on. We have to get a move on."

As it was, he wasn't going to get a proper breakfast. I grabbed a couple of granola bars for him to eat in the car that would hopefully tide him over until lunch. But when Finn came down the stairs, not only was he not ready to go, he was still in his pajamas.

"Mom," he croaked, his face flushed and a bit sweaty. "I'm really not feeling well. Can I stay home today? I just want to go back to sleep."

"Of course." I hurried up a few steps to meet him. When I laid the back of my hand on his face, his skin was warm and a little clammy. He also had dark circles under his eyes, making him look a little like a raccoon. While I wouldn't have thought Finn was warm enough to be considered 'feverish', he did look run down and overall, miserable. He'd been so quiet and distracted lately, I couldn't help but wonder if he was having trouble at school, and maybe that was the reason why he wanted to stay home.

He didn't look well, though, and he was

clearly exhausted—he obviously needed a break, for whatever reason. So, I smoothed his hair back off his sweaty forehead. "Finn… is everything okay?" I hesitated, because I'd asked him this question now over ten times. Whatever it was that was going on with him might have just been teenage stuff; not wanting to talk to his mom about everything, the first signs of independence. But I just couldn't quiet that worried little voice in the back of my head.

"You know you can talk to me about anything, right?" I meant every word. I'd do anything for my son and I hoped he knew that.

He looked at me, his face flushed. For a second, I thought he was going to spill whatever it was that was bothering him. But the moment passed, and he shook his head. "It's nothing. I just don't feel good. I'm really tired."

It was a struggle to hold back my disappointment, but I managed. "Okay. Do you want me to close the store today? I could stay home with you."

Finn shook his head. "I'll be okay. I'm just going to go back to sleep."

"Okay." I made myself smile. "You head back upstairs then, and I'll bring you some water and juice, okay?"

Finn nodded heavily, and then padded back up the stairs in his bare feet.

I couldn't push him to tell me more. That would just backfire. So, I grabbed a bottled water and a bottle of orange juice from the fridge. Something was clearly bothering my son, and I didn't have any idea what that something was. All I could do was hope he'd confide in me soon.

I took the drinks upstairs, and made sure Finn was tucked in and comfortable, and that his phone was in easy reach on the nightstand.

"I'll check in with you while I'm working at the store." I started fussing with his blankets and pillows, and I couldn't seem to make myself stop. "If you need anything, you just let me know and I'll be right back home, okay?"

Finn smiled, small, but genuine. "Okay, Mom. I'll be fine. Promise."

I hated to leave him. I wanted to stay, and make him soup, and to get him to talk to me. But from the way his blinks were getting longer and longer, he really was going to be asleep any second.

He'd be fine, I told myself. And he could reach me any time.

That didn't make it one ounce easier to leave him, though. I crossed my fingers that the day went by quickly.

Chapter Eleven

Of course, the store was dead all morning.

No customers to distract me, or make the time go by faster. And there were only so many times I could rearrange a shelf, or dust, or straighten things. I had some potions bubbling away in the back, but they were easy recipes that didn't require much thought. Being really distracted while brewing or working magic was such a terrible idea that I couldn't bring myself to work on any of the number of things that I could have been restocking.

Normally, the shop was a comfortable place for me. I'd built up Poppy's Potions with my own two hands, and everything from the heavy, old wooden shelves and display cases to the fairy lights and the multitude of rainbow-colored potion bottles filled me with pride as much as it relaxed me.

But today, all it did was put me on edge and reminded me that I wasn't home with my son.

It didn't help that Finn wasn't exactly quick to answer my texts every time I checked in on him. He apologized, and reminded me that he was just sleeping, but it didn't do anything for the anxiety churning in my stomach.

I knew if I let myself dwell on it, I was just going to work myself into a mess, and with no customers out on the street looking like they might want to come in and try out a potion or two, I was going to need to find a different distraction.

So, I picked up my phone, and after a minute of chewing my lower lip and hesitating, I dialed Andre's number.

Recent doubts aside, talking to Andre made me feel a lot better ninety-nine percent of the time. Just hearing his voice, with that thick, British accent, over the phone, was enough to have some of the tension easing out of my back.

"Poppy," he said, voice warm even across the line. "What can I do for you?"

And just like that, I felt like I could take a full breath again. Like if I tripped and stumbled, there would be hands reaching out to catch me.

"It's a slow day at the store, so I thought I'd

see what you were up to."

"Well," I heard the click of him putting something down on a table. Maybe a cup or a bowl. "I was actually working on a new trick, but it isn't going well, and I was just thinking I needed a distraction to get me out of my own head." His voice was wry, like he was laughing at himself. "And then you called. Isn't that... well, perfect timing?"

I had to laugh. It was odd, to be syncing up to someone else's moods like we were, but odd in a good way. I wished there was someone I could talk to about it. I didn't feel like I could approach Roy, with our history and with how snappy and on edge he'd been with everything lately. Fifi for the same reasons. But they were the only other people who were soulmates that I knew of, and the internet search I'd done had been even more disappointing than I'd expected.

"I'm sorry. I've just been worried about this whole," I waved my hand around. "Thing. And now Finn isn't feeling well, and he's sleeping, and I don't want to bother him, but he's not really answering my texts." I blew out a heavy sigh. "It's just, a lot, you know?"

"I do." I heard a bit of a creak over the line, like he was taking a seat. "I'm sure Finn will be fine. It's good for him to rest, if he's under the weather, right? There's a bit of a bug going around, I'm led to believe."

"I know I'm being ridiculous. Unfortunately, knowing that doesn't help me to stop being ridiculous."

"Poppy, you're not being ridiculous. You're worried about your son. I'd be concerned if you weren't."

The counter was digging into my spine where I was leaning against it, so I straightened up and turned around to face the front door instead. "Thank you. I'm just not sure what to do. I could close up the store and go home, but I don't want Finn to think I'm babying him or anything."

Whatever Andre said to that was lost in the spasm of panic that shot straight up my spine. Because facing the windows, I had a front row seat of Kenzie Chase: vlogger, influencer, and general pain in the neck, strolling up to the door of my shop, her phone already out and filming before she even set foot inside.

"Oh, God, Andre, I'll have to call you back. I've got a code blonde over here."

"A code what?"

I'd have to apologize later for hanging up on him, but the idea of even part of my conversation with Andre getting filmed and overheard by however many thousand followers made me sick to my stomach.

"And here we are in Haven Hollow's own quaint little potion shop, called Poppy's Potions." Kenzie smirked into her phone. "Here, they allegedly sell 'magic potions' to tourists, so it should be interesting to see if there's anything of substance." She turned her camera to pan the room. "Admittedly, it does look like it could be haunted... by the ghost of a nineteenth century dentist's office."

I tried not to bristle, knowing that Kenzie was just trying to get a reaction. From reading the group chat, she'd been getting more and more antagonistic to anyone she talked to, apparently trying to get them angry enough that they let something slip. It had been a good thing that Fifi was in the Half-Moon when Kenzie had breezed in, or Roy might have launched her straight out of town like a javelin.

That didn't keep her comments from hurting my feelings, though. I'd worked hard on my shop, and I was proud of what I'd accomplished here. I wasn't about to let a nasty girl with a camera tear it down.

Kenzie swung the camera my way. "Are you the owner of this place?"

The years might have been long behind me, but I'd been a twenty-something girl before. So, I recognized the gleam in Kenzie's eyes, like a coyote watching to see if their bite had drawn blood. A little girl acting up for an audience. She wanted me to flinch, to get defensive, she 'won' if I did.

So, even though I wanted to boot her behind right out the door, and maybe give her a piece of my mind in the process, I just slapped on my very best customer service smile and folded my hands on the counter. I would be the bigger person. "I'm Poppy, yes." And then I used the phrase that Henner had taught me, magic words to deal a mortal blow to the horrible little gremlin. "And I don't consent to being recorded."

Instantly, Kenzie's smirk disappeared and her face soured like spoiled milk. She glared at me as she shoved her phone back into her pocket. I'd have to thank Henner for that little nugget later.

She might still be recording, but with that one little phrase, she wouldn't be able to post any of it online or she'd risk getting sued. That would have to be good enough for now.

Her face still set in petulant lines, Kenzie glared around the store. Then she shot me a look. "Okay, but for real. The potion thing is just marketing, right? What are they actually, perfume? Essential oils?"

"There are essential oils in them, yes, and some do smell very nice. But no, they aren't perfume—just as the shop sign says—they're potions."

Kenzie rolled her eyes in the way that only those who had recently been teenagers could. "Okay, sure." She picked up one potion from a display in front of her. "Confidence," she read the label, before looking back at me. "So, what, I drink this, and it makes me feel more sure of myself, is that it? Nice placebo effect."

My smile got a little tighter, and my fingers twisted together. "I wouldn't suggest you drink it, unless you want some serious stomach issues. All my potions are meant to be worn on the skin. And as for that one, you could anoint your throat with it, especially if public speaking scares you."

She set the potion back down on the counter a little too hard, and I just barely held back my wince. "Sure. Let's see, potions for sleeping, potions for energy, potions for dreams. All nice and vague, so the power of suggestion can do its work. Typical." Then she snorted.

Against my will, a flush started in my chest and crept up my throat into my cheeks. And that power within me began to boil, began to leach from my core, down into my extremities and it was all I could do to keep a lid on it, to keep it under control. But I managed, thank God.

"It's not just the 'power of suggestion', actually. You–"

"So, what exactly about them makes them magic?" she asked, talking right on top of me. She picked up another bottle, a delicate purple one with a potion guaranteed to encourage sweet dreams inside. She popped the cork and took a curious sniff, lavender scent ghosting into the air. "Is magic one of the ingredients? Water from some mystic spring? A special cauldron, maybe?"

"No," I answered.

She smirked, and half-stuffed the topper back into the bottle, then set it carelessly back on the shelf. The bottle wobbled precariously, and I had to lunge out from behind the counter to catch it before it could shatter on the ground.

My heart shot up into my throat as I clutched the potion bottle, still not quite believing I'd caught it in time. The memory of the last time someone had dropped a potion in Haven Hollow was still pretty darn vivid. Yeah, sure, Wanda had gotten a pseudo daughter out of the deal, but the resulting explosion had also taken out the entire front of her store, and her shop window. I wasn't taking any chances.

"How about you head back out the door, since it's clear you're not interested in anything I sell."

Kenzie actually laughed.

The power hiding behind my rib cage fluttered and stirred, like something waking up from hibernation.

"No, but seriously." She leaned against my counter, rolling another potion bottle across the wooden surface negligently with two fingers. "Magic potions—this is a joke, right? Just something for the tourists? You must rake in the cash from naïve idiots. But props to you, I respect the hustle."

If I ground my teeth together any harder, I was worried I was going to wear my enamel down to dust. It took everything in me not to smack her hands away from the potion, or pluck it out of her loose grasp and set it back down safely. "Maybe you should try one before you dismiss them as a hoax, or a joke."

For someone who built up her brand chasing down paranormal events, Kenzie seemed to be a pretty hardcore skeptic. I wondered how much of this act she was putting on was just for her audience. But then I reminded myself that she couldn't post any of it. Could she post the audio? Hmm, I wasn't sure about that. I'd have to let Henner known asap so he could scrub anything she attempted to upload.

The bell above the door chimed, and Taliyah Morgan stepped into the store. She was wearing her glamor, so she looked like a no-nonsense, middle-aged woman with gray streaked hair and lines around her mouth and eyes.

Even through her sunglasses, I could tell she was glaring at Kenzie. “Miss Chase, I’ve been getting a number of reports about you harassing townspeople and local businesses. I’m not sure how things work wherever you come from, but we have rules and laws in this town and one of them states that you’re not permitted to interfere with people’s lives and their livelihood. Especially not for your little videos.”

“Well, she was just leaving,” I said and then gave Kenzie a look that said if she knew what was good for her, she’d do exactly that.

Instead, Kenzie scowled and crossed her arms. Her hip jutted to one side. “Oh, I get it.” She gave us both a narrow-eyed look. “You’re both in on it.”

“In on what?” Taliyah nearly spat the words at her.

“The conspiracy happening in this town. You’re just trying to shut me down.” She laughed, a nasty sound. “Well, it’s not going to work.”

“There is no conspiracy.” Taliyah’s face screwed up with the words, and I knew she hated to say them. She, and her brother before her, the previous Chief Morgan, had been convinced that there was a cult operating in town. It wasn't until Taliyah's seal broke that she learned the truth, and realized just what the town was hiding. Cain never had—well, not until he possessed Darla and learned the truth.

"You've already been warned, so now you need to move along, unless you'd like to spend the night behind bars. I don't think you'll find much there to amuse your followers."

Kenzie stalked towards the door, glaring at both of us. "You're probably being paid off by whoever's in charge around here."

I winced, and Taliyah's face darn near turned to stone. She didn't take accusations of corruption lightly, and by the way the temperature was dropping in the shop, she was about three seconds away from making Kenzie Chase regret her words.

Kenzie paused, her eyes wide and darting around as she held out her hands to either side of her. "Wait, do you feel that? It just got way colder in here! There might be a paranormal event occurring!"

She then fumbled for her phone, and I used the distraction to wipe a streak of frost off the counter.

"Out," Taliyah and I barked in unison. I even pointed towards the door.

So, potions were hokum, but ghosts and 'paranormal events' were real? Hmph.

Eventually, and with a lot of bad grace, Kenzie stalked out the door. "This isn't going to stop me. I'm going to get to the bottom of whatever is going on in this town."

"Keep doing what you're doing and the only thing you're going to get to the bottom of is your own jail cell," Taliyah answered.

The bell jangled angrily as Kenzie slammed the door, and then she was gone. I came out from around the counter to stand beside Taliyah as we watched the girl stalk off.

"Not that I'm not grateful for the rescue, but how did you know to show up?" Taliyah normally had really excellent timing, but this was a little bit too excellent, even for her.

"Andre called me," she said without looking at me. Her eyes were still plastered on Kenzie, who strode across Main Street, clearly heading for Wanda's Witchery. "He said you might need someone to scare off our brand-new nuisance."

A bubble of bright happiness rose up in my chest. I'd have to thank Andre the next time I spoke to him. Taliyah was exactly the person I'd needed, someone official enough to run Kenzie off without looking suspicious.

"Thank you." I watched a bit longer. Kenzie was definitely heading for Wanda's shop. "Um, should we stop her?"

A tiny little smirk curled Taliyah's mouth,

ruining her scary cop face. "Nah. Maverick's working today."

I could see the tall shadow of Wanda's cousin lurking just inside the door to the shop. He waited until Kenzie was just about in arm's reach of the door, and then he reached out, flipped the sign on the door to 'closed', and turned the lock in her face.

Kenzie gave the door a few futile tugs before scowling and storming off.

I, meanwhile, almost pulled something trying not to giggle. Even Taliyah seemed to be fighting back a laugh.

Then her phone rang, and after she answered it with a short, "Chief Morgan," her smile vanished like frost in the sun.

Chapter Twelve

Since Taliyah stalked out without *expressly* telling me not to follow her, I flipped the sign to closed, locked up, and hurried out of the store after her.

She must have been okay with that, because she just grunted when I caught up with her.

"Is everything okay?" I asked, slightly out of breath from jogging to keep up with her longer stride.

Taliyah's mouth tightened. "There's been another incident."

I winced, giving a furtive look around to see if Kenzie was still in the area, but I didn't see even a glimpse of blonde hair, so she must have found someone else to terrorize. "Is whatever the object is big? Maybe we should call Roy, in case we need help moving it?"

A complicated series of expressions passed over Taliyah's face, until it finally settled on tired and stressed. "I don't think that's going to be possible."

She wouldn't say any more until we reached her cruiser.

"I'm coming with you," I said as I reached for the passenger door.

"Suit yourself."

A short drive later, I understood what she meant with a sinking heart.

Trellway fountain had existed pretty much since Haven Hollow was founded. It was the centerpiece of one of the larger parks in the area, with its three tiers and sparkling white basin. People liked to throw coins in it, thinking doing so brought them good luck. I didn't know much about the luck part, but I'd always enjoyed seeing it whenever Finn and I stopped in to play frisbee, or have a little picnic dinner when the weather was nice.

Normally, the fountain filled me with a soothing calm—listening to the cheerful burble of the water trickling down from its tiered basins. But all I felt at the moment was dread when I caught sight of the white stone which had been turned to brilliant gold.

It wasn't just the fountain itself that had

turned to gold, either. The water in the basins, and a thin jet of it rising into the air, had also solidified into a gaudy, shining mess. The whole thing, top to bottom, was now gold. Thank goodness the park wasn't normally busy at this time of day, or there would have been a gaggle of people clustered around, taking more pictures and posting them online, and drawing the attention of a persistent blonde vlogger.

Instead, there was only one woman waiting anxiously by the north entrance of the park, with her little dog that was sniffing here and there, completely unconcerned. I'd seen this particular woman around town before, but I'd never spoken to her. As she stood there, she wrung her hands together and reminded me a bit of a mushroom; short, stocky, with a cap of sleek white hair and watery pale eyes. She was bundled up in a thick pink coat, even though it really wasn't that cool outside.

Her dog looked a bit like a bristle brush. He was a tiny thing, with his coarse, dark hair sticking out at every angle—not like he was unkempt, but more that his fur seemed to have picked a direction and grown that way. He looked like a big guinea pig, until he raised his little muzzle from the ground, and his little ears perked up. And that little face was enough to warm anyone's heart.

As soon as we were in range, the woman started babbling.

"I'm so sorry to trouble you, your Highness —"

Taliyah raised a hand. "Please, call me Chief Morgan."

The woman nodded. "Well, Chief Morgan, I didn't know who else to call. All sorts of humans use this park, and I know there's been trouble lately, and this... well, this is beyond my ability to fix."

Clearly, the woman, whatever court or flavor, was a faerie. No one else would ever call Taliyah by her winter court title.

"You did the right thing, Dottie. Thank you for calling."

Dottie's slightly pasty cheeks flushed pink. The little dog eyed us, and deciding that I was probably not a threat to him and his owner, squared up to Taliyah. He let out a squeaky little growl, and Dottie immediately scooped him up, holding him close to her chest.

"Reginald," she scolded. "Be polite to Chief Morgan."

Reginald didn't look repentant in the least.

Taliyah, meanwhile, eyed the fountain like it was radioactive. Then she swept her suit jacket back with her wrists as she propped her hands on her hips, putting her badge on display either deliberately or through habit. “When did you first notice the fountain?”

Dottie chewed her thick bottom lip. “Well, Reginald and I like to come here in the mornings, early, so about eight o’clock?”

“Eight?” Taliyah turned to stare at her. “That was hours ago. Why did you wait so long to call?”

Dottie blanched, all the color draining back out of her cheeks. She clutched Reginald to her chest, and the little dog sneezed at Taliyah.

“I’m so sorry. I didn’t want to be a bother. And I thought that maybe the fountain would just turn back on its own, some things have turned to gold have turned back on their own, you know. But then it didn’t, and there are a lot of people here in the afternoons, especially once the school lets out, and I wasn’t sure what to do.”

She was right. We weren’t far from Finn’s school and school would be over in about fifteen minutes. Probably a hundred kids would soon be cutting through the park on their way home. Finn would have been one of them—well, if he weren’t home sick, that is. And on that note, I glanced at my phone as discretely as I could. There was still no answer from my last text, and a jittery, anxious feeling was coiling tighter in my stomach.

It was pretty obvious that Taliyah was counting to ten in her head, trying not to snap. I thought if she said a harsh word to Dottie, the older woman might actually wither up and blow away.

"I understand," Taliyah said carefully. "But the longer this... gold fountain is out in the open, the more likely it is that someone else will stumble across it. Human someone elses. And then we've got a real mess on our hands."

Dottie visibly brightened, setting Reginald back down on the ground where he took up a protective stance in front of her. "Oh! No, I know, that's why I hid it."

I glanced between Taliyah and the beaming Dottie. Taliyah seemed to be having a moment, so I asked, hesitantly. "Hid it?"

She nodded so hard that her white hair flew around her face. "Yes, I hid the fountain."

Taliyah and I both turned and looked at the huge, gleaming, obvious gold fountain that was still squatting in the middle of the park. It wasn't very hidden. At all.

"You did?" Taliyah asked, her voice dry.

That seemed to fluster Dottie a little. "Oh, well, not from you two, obviously. But I hid it from the humans."

I was arguably human, but I guessed I had enough magic not to be included in that category. But I didn't see any barriers, or arcane symbols like Wanda or the rest of the coven might have used to hide such an enormous object. Dottie hadn't even thrown a big blanket over it or anything similar. "Hid it how?"

Dottie smiled, a small, secret smile, and she leaned forward like she was going to impart some important secret to us. "I'm very good at not being noticed. And when I work at it, I can make it so that people don't notice other things, either. I've been standing here, hiding the fountain ever since I found it. No one else has seen it. I promise."

Taliyah nodded, looking impressed and a little relieved. "Thank you, Dottie. That was good work."

Dottie beamed.

Pulling out her phone, Taliyah started typing. "Can you keep hiding the fountain for a bit longer, Dottie?"

Dottie's head tilted to one side, like she was really thinking about it. Then she nodded. "For a while longer. Not too much, though. I'm very tired."

"Okay, thank you." Taliyah finished her message, and slipped the phone away again. "I've told the others what's going on, and I asked Wanda to hurry up and get here. We need the coven to handle this as soon as possible."

The sun was still high in the sky, resting in the cloudless blue stretch like an accusation. “Wanda won’t be able to come for hours, yet. It’s daylight still.”

Dottie cupped her cheeks. “Well, the sun won’t set for a couple more hours.” Then she worried her lower lip. “Oh, dear, that’s quite a while for me to continue.”

“Wanda’s going to have to risk it.” Taliyah turned to glare at the fountain like it had personally offended her. “Dottie can’t hold the area until sunset. And once Wanda gets here, Dottie, you can return home.” Then she took a breath as something else occurred to her. “Dottie, could you manage to hide the fountain and a witch?”

“Yes, I could.”

It wasn’t a great solution, but I had to admit it was the only one we had at the moment. I just hoped that Wanda’s nocturnal restrictions didn’t cause problems for her down the line. Thinking about it, I checked the vicinity for any sign of a nosy, old vampire woman but didn’t see anyone.

Wanda must have realized that Taliyah was rapidly reaching the end of her rope about the whole gold situation, because she didn’t even put up much of an argument when Taliyah phoned her. Maverick arrived shortly after Taliyah sent out the call, with Imani, Betanya, and Olga arriving in Imani's car.

I was just starting to wonder how Wanda was going to get herself to the park, when a big black hearse drove down the road.

Lorcan was an older vampire, and he'd had a few near misses in his youth, to hear him talk about it. When someone is unconscious and unable to do much of anything to defend themselves while the sun was in the sky, they learned to get creative about their resting place. That meant Lorcan had multiple properties, and no real schedule for when he slept and where, but his other option was the hearse. It came complete with a coffin in the back, and he could doze away the daytime hours while being constantly moved around town.

It was Marty that he'd hired to be the hearse's driver. When he was out and about running errands, he'd just drive the big car around with a sleeping vampire in the back. And I could see him through the windshield, lifting his hand for a cheerful wave as he carefully brought the hearse up over the curb and trundled over the grass towards us.

"Does he have to do that?" Taliyah asked, motioning to the grass. "I'm sure I'm going to hear about it later."

"Bigger fish to fry, Taliyah," I reminded her, and she begrudgingly agreed.

When he came to a stop, he leapt out of the car and hurried around to the back to help Wanda out of the coffin. No one was particularly surprised to see the witch emerging from a vampire's coffin, except for maybe Dottie, who'd picked up Reginald again, hugging the little dog to her chest.

Wanda, a bit ruffled from her ride in the coffin, ran a hand through her hair and glared at the fountain like she was thinking of hexing it out of existence and calling it a day.

"A fountain," she finally snapped, gesturing angrily. "Who the spell turns a *fountain* to gold? What's the point?"

I shrugged and wrapped my arms around my uneasy stomach. My magic was roiling again, pressing against my ribs like it was testing the give. "Maybe they wanted to see if they could turn liquid into gold?" I offered weakly.

Wanda glared at me and then turned back to glare at the fountain. "Let's get this over with," she muttered as she stalked up the slight hill to reach the bottom basin.

While the witches got set up, discussing who should stand where and what the plan was, Marty sidled up to Taliyah and me. My heart gave a bruised little beat that there wasn't any hesitation, no flinching around the edges of his smile when he looked at me. I'd been clinging to my hope that we could get back to where we'd been, that we could be friends again, and I didn't want to do anything to ruin it.

"Hey, Tally," Marty said, getting away with the nickname only because he was Taliyah's cousin. "I was going to call you, actually. The other day, when you mentioned people having gold stuff go missing. Was any of it weird food statues?"

Taliyah paused, her brow wrinkling above the line of her sunglasses. "Food statues? No. Why do you ask?"

He turned back towards the hearse, and waved for us to follow. "So, I had to make a run to the dump. A piece of equipment that we were using on our haunt busts, it…" he coughed, turning a bit pink. "Well, anyway, it broke. So, I took what was left of it down to throw away, and while I was there, I found these under some bags."

He opened the passenger side of the hearse, and sitting in the footwell, was a pile of solid gold... well, food. I gaped. There had to be thousands of dollars in gold there, and someone had just thrown it into the trash?

Taliyah took her pen out of her pocket, poking at the pieces and rolling them around so she could see each piece better. "No, none of these are the pieces missing. It was all jewelry from the jewelry store and antiques from Timeless Treasures."

Marty's shoulders drooped. "Well, dang. I guess you should take these, though, in case whoever got rid of them wants them back."

"Hold on a second." I crouched, looking at the pieces more carefully.

Now, people do some weird things when it comes to home decorating. If the bits had been all artful fruit pieces, or even, I don't know, an oyster shell, that would have made more sense. But a handful of gold french fries? And a gold burger, with what looked like a partial bite taken out of it? A gold *Coke*? That was a little out there, even for kitsch.

My stomach went cold as the realization started to sink in, and I clasped a hand over my mouth in horror. "Oh, *no*."

Taliyah was instantly alert. "Poppy?"

Marty put a hand on my shoulder. "You okay, Pops?"

Even the little thrill of relief I got from hearing my old nickname again couldn't fight back the feeling of dread snaking along my spine. "The food, well... it's food, don't you get it?"

From the looks they gave me, they didn't.

"We thought that whoever it is was turning things to gold to draw attention or pull a prank." My words were coming out so fast, they were tripping over each other. I waved at the pile of glittering metal. “It’s not a prank. We’re dealing with a King Midas type curse, I think. Everything this person touches turns to gold. And that means—well, that they can’t eat, Taliyah, or their food turns to gold when they pick it up.”

I looked at the fountain in horror, new understanding showing me a very different picture. “They picked the fountain because they were trying to get the *water*. They needed to drink it.”

Taliyah looked grim, her mouth pressed into a tight line. “It’s been a few days now; if that’s true, that means they’ve got to be in rough shape.”

“We need to find them. We need to find them before…” I shook my head. I couldn’t even finish the sentence.

“Let me talk to Wanda.” Taliyah stalked off up the hill, leaving behind a little patch of frost that quickly melted even in the weak sunlight.

All I could do was shake my head. We’d been so annoyed, so put out, and all the while, a person was suffering. I felt terrible. When the tree was turned back to wood, the person must have thought the curse was gone, only to touch it again and have it turn to gold a second time. That must have been devastating.

“It’s okay, Pops.” Marty laid a big hand on

my shoulder, and gave me a little comforting squeeze. “You’ll figure it out. I know you will.”

It was hard not to cry, but I was just so darn grateful to have Marty in my life again. I was so happy that maybe, just maybe, we might find our way back to each other again. Some day?

“Thanks, Marty.” I gave him a smile I hoped wasn’t too watery around the edges. “And thanks again for doing hot dog night with Finn the other day. He really loves hanging out with you.”

Marty’s forehead creased, his brows almost touching together in puzzlement. “I mean, of course I’m always happy to have Finn over. We like the same video games, and he’s really good at them. But he hasn’t been over in a few weeks now.”

“What?” I shook my head, my stomach dropping down to my toes. “He said he was going to see you the other night?”

Marty frowned and shook his head. “He didn’t.”

“But you dropped him off at my house—I saw you?”

Marty, if anything, looked more confused. “He asked me to pick him up. He said he had some project he was working on with a group of other kids, and that you had to work late, and would I give him a ride home.” He shrugged.

“It wasn’t any trouble. But I only saw him for the ride.”

My stomach flipped over. Finn had lied to me? Why wouldn’t he have just told me he needed to work on a project? Unless there was no project at all, and he was covering for something else? What in the world was going on with my son?

“Oh, okay. Thanks Marty.” I pulled out my phone, trying to keep my breathing steady. Still no response from Finn from my last text. I tried again, telling him to call me right away. I forced myself to wait a full minute, and when he still hadn’t answered me, I called his phone. It immediately sent me to voicemail, and my heart leapt from a jog into a sprint. Something was wrong. I knew it.

My hands were shaking so hard as I jogged towards Marty’s hearse that I almost couldn’t hit the right buttons, but I managed to pull up Andre’s contact, and he, at least, answered on the second ring.

“Poppy? What’s wrong?”

He must have been getting echoes of my rising panic along our bond. I closed my eyes, trying to hold the tears back. They wouldn’t help. I needed to focus. “I think something’s wrong, but I’m not sure what. Finn stayed home sick today, but he isn’t answering my calls or texts.

Is there any way that you can pop over to the house to check on him?" My phone case creaked as my grip tightened. "I'm sorry to bother you, I just need to know what's going on, but you're closer, and–"

"Poppy," Andre said, cutting through my shaky babbling. "Of course. I'll go now. I'll call you back as soon as I get there, okay?"

"Okay." I let out a trembling breath. "Okay. Thank you."

It was only after I hung up that I realized I hadn't even thanked him for sending Taliyah my way earlier. One crisis at a time and this crisis was a way more important one because it involved my son. I shoved my phone into my purse and wrenched the car door open. "Marty, I need you to take me home as soon as possible, if you wouldn't mind?"

"Of course," he answered.

Taliyah beckoned me over towards the fountain, but I didn't have time for gold curses, not when I didn't know what was going on with my son.

"Sorry, I have to go. Family emergency," I called out as I all but threw myself into the hearse.

Taliyah might be one heck of a police Chief, but she was also a mom. She might not be thrilled about me abandoning an investigation, but she'd understand that kids came first, always.

At least focusing on Marty driving kept me from focusing on the anvil in my stomach. When my phone rang halfway back to the farmhouse, it was a darn good thing I'd hooked it up to the car's bluetooth, or I might have driven off the road trying to fumble it out of my bag again.

"Hello? Andre?" I was clutching the door handle so tightly that all the blood had blanched out of my fingers, leaving them stark white against the gray leather. I didn't even realize I was now talking to my new boyfriend in front of my old one.

I could tell the second Andre started talking that something was wrong. "Poppy, I think you need to come to the house. Finn isn't here. I looked everywhere, including out back, but he's gone."

A terrible, icy calm settled over me. The power that had been sloshing against the inside of my ribcage, went deathly still, like the calm before the sky tore open and poured its fury across the world.

"I'm on my way," was all I said.

And then Marty stomped the gas pedal all the way to the floor.

Chapter Thirteen

Breaking several traffic laws, we managed to get home in less than five minutes.

"Do you need me to help?" Marty asked.

I looked at him and remembered Andre was at the farmhouse and Wanda still needed Marty to take her home. "No," I managed with as nice a smile as I could muster. "In fact, Wanda will need you to take her home, but thank you so much."

He just nodded. "Please let me know when you find Finn."

I jumped out of the hearse and nodded to him. "I will." Then I was pelting up the driveway and into the house. Andre met me at the front door, his expression grim. There was a tightness to the skin around his eyes, and I could tell without him saying a word that he was as worried for Finn as I was.

"I checked all the rooms," he started, matching my stride as I raced through the house. "I even poked down into the basement a bit, checked the cemetery out back, but I couldn't find any sign of him."

It wasn't that I didn't believe Andre, I was sure he really had done a thorough search of the old house. It was more that I couldn't stop myself from methodically going over every nook and cranny—just to make sure Finn really wasn't here. And yes, I even checked the old, creepy, fieldstone basement that neither Finn nor I cared to spend any time in. I managed to keep it together enough to note that Finn's pajamas from that morning were draped over his laundry hamper, and his shoes were missing from the front hall. I checked the back door and noticed his bike was gone. So that had to mean that he'd gotten dressed and headed out. But where could he have gone?

Andre came with me as I walked out the back door to the small cemetery behind the house. But no, Andre was correct again—there was no sign of Finn. And that meant one thing: my son was missing. I had no idea where he was, or why he'd gone wherever he'd gone to, or why he wasn't answering my many texts and phone calls. As far as I could tell, his phone was turned off, because it was now sending me directly to voicemail.

I needed to find him.

I grabbed one of my larger bags, the one I used when we were going out and likely to need drinks and snacks and sunscreen and the like. Then I started grabbing every potion in the house that I thought might prove useful, and stuffed them into the bag. *Uncrossing Oil*? In the bag. A banishment potion? In the bag. *Fiery Command Oil*? You'd better believe it was going in the bag.

Once the thing was practically bulging at the seams, I hooked the strap over my chest with the bag under my arm like a holster. Then I turned back to Andre, who'd been at my heels and careful not to get in my way. As soon as he noticed the bulging bag though, he immediately reached over and pulled it off my shoulder, placing it on his. I didn't argue.

"Okay." I took a breath, trying to ignore the way my hands were trembling, nerves or adrenaline, I couldn't tell. "Can you give me a ride back to my Jeep at my shop?"

"Of course."

"I'm going to search Haven Hollow for him, starting with his friends' houses."

He nodded. "What can I do?"

"Can you check any public places you can think of? Sweeter Haunts, or even Stomper's Creamery?"

He just nodded, carried my bag of potions to his Range Rover, opened the passenger door, and plopped them on the floor before he turned to face me, his car keys already in his hand.

"I'll check the arcade, too. Maybe some of the bigger parks."

The mention of the parks reminded me of Taliyah and Wanda who were still at the golden fountain. I hesitated for a split second, but dragged my phone out again. It wasn't that I didn't think the fountain and protecting Haven Hollow was important, of course it was. But the fountain was gold and couldn't get hurt. And the more people looking for Finn, the better the odds of finding him quickly.

I'd just unlocked my phone, ready to dial, when it started ringing in my hand.

Finn.

I almost dropped the phone in my hurry to answer it. "Finn? Are you okay? Where are you?"

"Mom?" The shaky, teary sound of his voice had my heart clenching painfully tight. "Mom, I messed up. I was trying to fix it, but it got way worse instead and now it's out of control and people are in trouble."

I shoved away my own panic, my voice eerily calm when I spoke. "Finn, breathe for me, okay? Everything is going to be just fine, I promise. But you need to tell me where you are so I can come and get you. And then we'll get everything sorted out, okay? Where are you?"

I heard him taking a few breaths across the line. "I'm at school."

I blinked, surprised, and glanced at Andre, who was tense and ready to move. "At school?"

Why would he pretend to be sick in order to stay home, only to end up going back to school, anyway? Granted, school was already out by this time, but the whole thing was still bizarre.

"Yeah." He sounded so young, and lost. It broke my heart. "Hurry, okay?"

I was already moving, and Andre was quick behind me as he jumped into the driver's seat while I remained on the phone with Finn. "Andre and I on our way, okay? Just make sure you're somewhere safe and we'll be there in a couple minutes."

If I'd thought Marty had bent the traffic laws into pretzels to get me here, Andre just flat out ignored them. His driving never felt unsafe or out of control, but at times I was forcibly reminded that, in London, they drove on the opposite side of the road.

I stayed on the phone with Finn for the entire drive, narrating exactly where we were, how close we were getting, and I listened as he tried to breathe, to calm himself down, and I wanted to claw my way through the phone to be at his side so badly that it scared me a little.

When we screeched into the parking lot, Finn was waiting outside the school gym. The parking lot was basically empty, but there were a few loiterers who were getting picked up. I barely had time to jump out of the car and shove my phone away before Finn was wrapped around me like a limpet, clinging tight.

“I’m sorry,” he half sobbed against my shoulder. “I really messed up. I didn’t think anyone could get hurt. I’m sorry, Mom.”

My son was okay, safe in my arms, if upset. But I gave myself that one moment, to just clutch him to me and really feel that he was okay, in one piece, and anything else could just wait for a second while I convinced my heart to ease back down out of my throat and stop trying to choke me.

Andre put the Range Rover in park and walked around it and as soon as Finn noticed him, he released me and threw his arms around Andre, who immediately held him and rubbed his back as he said in his soft voice, “It’s all going to be okay, my boy. Just breathe and tell us what happened and together, your mother and I will fix whatever it is."

Finn pulled away from him then and, looking up, nodded as Andre smiled down at him. Then Finn took a deep breath and wiped his nose on his sleeve and faced me.

"Okay, buddy, now tell us what's going on," I whispered.

"Instead of telling you, I need to show you," he answered and then turned around before looking back at me with a little wave. "Come on, we have to hurry." He turned, heading back towards the school, but reached out and grabbed my hand, as if afraid he'd lose me.

Andre then returned to his car, grabbed my bag of potions and caught up to us, the bottles clinking together lightly, his long legs easily keeping pace.

"Mr. Lannister, he's my science teacher," Finn started. "And he's always been a bit of a grump." Finn turned a corner, leading us down another hallway. "But lately he's been really picking on my friend, Sophie."

"You mentioned something similar," I said. "I remember."

He looked at me and nodded. "I don't get it. She's not a bad student. She's super smart and always aces her tests. Plus, she's nice, and really quiet. But... well, he really started being extra mean to her after she told him what her science fair project was."

Finn was a very gifted young man. He was a budding Magician, and he could tell when a person was lying, but this conversation just revealed how young he still was in that he hadn't considered that some adults were just mean, or jealous, or petty. Bullies weren't strictly teenagers.

We turned down the main hallway, and I realized we were heading for the front office.

"Sophie's parents are botanists," he continued. "Anyway, I told you how her project was grafting a branch from an orange tree to an apple tree, so that the tree would grow both fruits?"

"Yes, I recall," I answered.

Through the office doors, I realized that the secretary who usually ruled from behind her desk, was absent which was just as well. In fact, the hallways had been eerily quiet. Finn hurried towards the closed door of the principal's office.

"And it was working—the tree was growing both sorts of fruits, apples and oranges," Finn said, indignant. Still full of the belief that people should be fair. "And she had all these scientific papers to back her up. But Mr. Lannister just kept telling her that only dummies would believe that apples could 'turn into' oranges.

That one thing can't turn into another."

He paused then, in front of the door. His hands twisted together, skin blanching white from his grip. He was so angry, he was shaking.

"It was like he just didn't want Sophie to do well. And I wanted to prove him wrong, to make him stop. So… so I kind of… made a potion."

"Wait, what?" I shook my head as everything started to make a horrible kind of sense. "You made a potion?"

Finn nodded, looking miserable. "I've seen you do it hundreds of times. Thousands. And I have magic, too, so I thought if I just followed the recipe, your recipe…" He took a big, gulping breath. "Anyway. I made *Gypsy Gold*, Mom, just like you did for Andre. And then I used it to turn a pencil into pyrite. I just wanted to stump Mr. Lannister, to make him realize he was wrong about Sophie and her project. It was just supposed to be a prank," he trailed off, staring at the floor.

"Finn," I said, absolutely appalled. "That is *not* a prank. And you know better than to show magic to a mundane! That isn't okay."

"Bad business, Finn," Andre said quietly, shaking his head. "It never ends well for anyone."

"I know. I know I screwed up." Finn blinked

rapidly, his eyes shiny. “But Mr. Lannister, he freaked out. He grabbed the pencil, and he kept turning it around and looking at it—like he was trying to find something wrong with it. And then he stormed out of the fair! With him gone, the other judges were a lot nicer, and Sophie ended up taking first place like she should have.”

“But?” I started.

Finn’s shoulders slumped, and he raked a hand back through his hair. “But then the next day, Mr. Lannister was even meaner, mostly towards Sophie, like she’d done something personally to upset him. And he’s been getting worse, and then he started missing classes. Well, one day last week, he was so awful to Sophie, he made her cry. So, I went to the principal to see if he could make Mr. Lannister stop. And the principal said he’d talk to him, and, well…”

Finn turned the knob, and the door to the principal’s office swung open slowly.

And there sat the school principal, Mr. Stillwater, who had been turned entirely into gold.

Chapter Fourteen

"Bloody hell," Andre said as we both tried to make sense of what was facing us.

I took a staggered step into the office, staring at the principal, or what used to be the principal, in horror.

I knew Mr. Stillwater. I'd seen him at PTA meetings and fundraisers. He'd reached out to me last year when he'd thought Finn was cutting classes, and he'd let me know that something was very wrong when the Magicless had attacked, posing as a teacher. He was a good man, and good at his job.

And he was frozen stiff, gold lips still parted as he tapped the desk blotter with a golden finger. Like he'd been frozen into place mid-sentence.

How could something like this have happened? *Gypsy Gold* was a party trick, a tiny, harmless little enchantment. It didn't turn men into statues, or terrorize a town.

Unless… unless a budding Magician, still new to his power, tried to channel his power into a potion instead of into a Magician's tricks. I'd seen firsthand what happened when different types of magic came together unexpectedly. Like when Wanda had spilled a potion on a bit of enchanted embroidery that her Blood Warlock cousin had been working on. Blended magic could do bizarre, unexpected things—like make a person out of a mannequin. Or curse a nasty teacher with the Midas touch.

Finn twisted his hands in the bottom of his sweatshirt, his eyes glassy as he fought not to cry again. "I'm sorry. I know I screwed up. I never meant to hurt anyone."

His voice broke on the last word, and he angrily scrubbed at his eyes with his sleeve. I wanted to hug him so badly, but that would have to wait. I wasn't sure how long the principal would be okay in his gold coating, if he was okay at all. Andre set my bag on the desk, as my thoughts raced while I tried to think of what I could do.

"But, Mom—there's more." Finn grabbed hold of my arm. His face was so pale, his freckles looked like sepia ink on the bridge of his nose.

"Tell us everything," Andre said, his tone still soft.

Finn looked up at him and nodded. "Mr. Lannister was really angry when he came out of the principal's office. He forced Sophie into a classroom, and then he locked the door. And I couldn't get inside. I don't know what's going on, but I'm sure she needs help, and I don't know what to do."

"Did he touch Sophie?" I asked.

Finn shook his head. "He just forced her to go with him by yelling at her."

Okay, that was good.

My mama bear mode surged to the front of my brain. A child in possible peril? We needed to get her out of that room, pronto. But first, I needed to see what could be done for Mr. Stillwater, since I didn't have any idea how long he could survive being gold.

I just hoped we weren't already too late.

"Any ideas?" I asked Andre, hoping he was less out of his depth than I was.

My heart sank when he raked his hands back through his hair, staring at poor Mr. Stillwater with a question in his eyes. "Honestly, I haven't the foggiest idea of what in the world to do about this. I've never seen anything like it."

"Me neither." I bit my lip, rolling the flesh between my teeth. "Finn, has anyone else seen what happened to the principal?"

Finn shook his head. "No, it happened after school let out."

"But there are still teachers here right?"

"Yeah, I mean... I guess so."

At least this had happened after hours—I couldn't imagine the panic that would have ensued had it occurred during school. "Can you lock the door please?" I asked Finn who immediately went to do just that.

Then I faced Mr. Stillwater and took a deep breath. Well, a Midas curse was still a type of curse, right? So maybe what we needed was a bit of curse-breaking oil.

I grabbed for one of my vials of *Uncrossing Oil* and crossed my fingers as I smeared it liberally all over Mr. Stillwater's face. His skin was hard and cool under my fingers, but the gold warmed quickly from my body heat. I took that as a good sign and spread more oil down his neck.

Hands and feet were next, and all the while, I prayed the oil would work—that it would do something—or undo something, as the case may be. This certainly wasn't what the potion was intended for, not really, but a curse was a curse (I hoped), no matter how unwittingly it might have been laid.

It needed to work. It *had* to work.

I stood back and watched, searching for any hint of change in the gold principal. My heart was pounding along with the obnoxiously ticking second hand on the old black and white clock hanging on the wall. My skin started buzzing with the need to move, to get to Sophie. Who knew what was going on in the classroom. Who knew if Mr. Lannister had also turned her to gold.

The seconds ticked by, each one landing like the stab of a needle.

There wasn't any change in Mr. Stillwater.

It wasn't working.

Okay, I needed to call Wanda. If my potions weren't working, that meant I needed witch magic. But Wanda was still at the park, assuming Marty hadn't taken her home again. Furthermore, she'd need to use the hearse to get to the school, and who knew how much longer Mr. Stillwater had.

Finn, apparently realizing how bad this situation was getting, let out a little sob, but he tried to muffle it behind his hands. Andre reached over and cupped his shoulder, pulling Finn into him and then wrapped his arm around Finn, who started to quietly sob once more.

No, no, no, we didn't have time for this. We

didn't have time for Wanda and the coven to get here. I couldn't stand around, watching my son stare at the face of a man who'd become a statue, however accidentally. I didn't want him blaming himself.

Something had to work.

I tore through my bag, looking over the potions that I'd brought with me, but came up empty. I couldn't command Mr. Stillwater to not be gold, and banishing him might just send him back to his house. There had to be something. *Anything.*

"Give me your hand, Finn," Andre said as Finn nodded and together, they approached Mr. Stillwater. "Do you recall the trick you learned for replacing something after making it invisible?"

Finn nodded. "Do you think that will work?"

Andre swallowed hard. "I don't know, but it's worth a shot."

Finn nodded again and they performed the trick, calling out the words in unison, but the only thing that happened was that Mr. Stillwater disappeared for a moment, before reappearing again and he was just as gold as he had been.

Finn made a little broken sound, so quiet, but so full of grief that it felt like a knife slotting up between my ribs. Just gutting. Tears burned at the corners of my eyes, my breath coming heavier.

Deep down inside my chest, something broke with a small crack.

Power then suffused my body, slow and languid, like a cat stretching after it had been curled up somewhere small and snug. That magic slunk through my body, pushing its way between my ribs, through my blood, out into my hands.

The power was too big, too strong to contain it. It felt like it would push me apart to make room for itself, cracking me open like an egg.

It should have been terrifying. I'd never felt power like this before. I was strong, probably one of the best potion makers in town, which wasn't a small brag, since some of the others had literal centuries of experience on me. But my power was of bubbling elixirs and gentle moonlight. Of flowers, and oils and green growing things.

The magic moving through me now was something completely different. It felt like tidal waves and thunderstorms, graveyard dirt and the silvery glow of a full moon. Faintly, the taste of blood lingered at the back of my mouth, bright and metallic.

It wasn't Gypsy magic. It was something else. It felt almost like witch magic, but not quite. There was death to it, blood to it, hunger to it. It wasn't witch magic, no. Or rather, not *just* witch magic.

It felt a bit like all the witches I knew. Like Wanda's wild blood magic, Imani's bright prayers. Like Betanya's thoughtful deliberation, Olga's passion, and Maverick's shadowy strength. But there was some of Lorcan in there too—his blood—the same blood that lived in Wanda's veins. It felt like all of them all bound together, but it also felt like me—I could taste the crispness of morning dew beneath the flow of molten lava. I'd gotten the magic through the coven bonds, but as it sat, maturing in my bones, it had somehow, bafflingly, become mine, too.

It felt like a storm raging through my body. Strands of my hair blew around my face, caught on a wind that came from nowhere, but still swirled through the windowless office. I pulled in a shaky breath, and thunder rolled up my spine.

"Mom?" Finn asked, his voice wobbly as he watched the change overtake me.

"Poppy?" Andre echoed, and there was concern in his eyes.

But I couldn't respond. I couldn't speak. I was completely in my power's grasp. This was wild magic, a force of nature. I didn't know how to tame it, much less how to control it. I wasn't a witch, I didn't know how to twist a spell. All I knew was potions.

My eyes fell on my bag.

I still had a bottle of *Uncrossing Oil.*

My fingers were trembling, and I struggled not to drop or crush the delicate glass in my hand. Inside the cheerfully yellow vial, I could feel the spark of power that I put into all my potions, the one ingredient that made them more than essential oils and extracts. *Uncrossing Oil* was meant to break curses, to help people, to keep them safe from magic that would hurt them. That was what I needed, and I needed it really, really badly.

I caught that little flicker of magic and cupped it between my palms. My eyes slid closed, but I could still see that little spark, glowing like an ember from a fire in my hands. I took a deep breath, trying to calm my whirling thoughts, and the storm of magic raging inside me paused, listening.

"Is she okay?" I heard Finn whisper.

"Trust her," Andre answered and, even though my eyes were closed, I could hear the smile on his lips.

I breathed power into that little ember that lit within me, whispering to it.

Break the curse. Save him. Undo this harm that has been done. Bring him back. Save him.

I poured all of it into that fragile little vial of glass, and then I opened my eyes to see the potion inside blazing like a captive star was cupped between my hands.

"Mom?" Finn's voice sounded so thin and small.

I still couldn't speak. The magic had filled my lungs with power, and there was no air left for words. Two steps forward, and I was right in front of Principal Stillwater again. One more big breath, and a quick prayer to anyone who was listening, and I poured the potion on top of his golden head.

The *Uncrossing Oil* flowed over the metal, running down Mr. Stillwater's face, his shoulders, dripping down his body and somehow coating every inch of him. It didn't make sense. There wasn't that much liquid in the little potion bottle, but somehow the liquid was defying the laws of science and was multiplying, was spreading all over the man, to encompass every inch of him.

When the last two drops fell off Principal Stillwater's outstretched finger, a strange shimmer rolled over his body.

Slowly, so slowly that at first, I thought I was imagining it, but the longer I watched, the more the gold thinned, lightening to pale skin. A finger twitched. Then a shoulder. Mr. Stillwater blinked, gold flaking away, and then he sucked in a deep breath and started to cough.

"Oh my gosh," Finn whispered.

"You're doing it, Poppy," Andre said.

Yes, I was doing it.

The magic went out like a snuffed candle then, dropping me back into myself with an almost audible thud. I staggered, sweat dripping down the side of my face and my lungs heaving like I'd just run an entire marathon. Andre was instantly by my side, his arm around me, and I fell into him, feeling suddenly exhausted. No, it was more than that—I felt hollowed out, like I'd been scraped clean on the inside, and my muscles were shivering.

"Is my mom okay?" Finn asked.

"I'm... I'm fine, buddy," I finally managed, even as I wondered if such were the case. Once I could stand on my own, Andre released me and hurried to Mr. Stillwater's side, trying to help him calm his breathing before he choked. Suddenly, my son's arms were around me and he was clinging to me so tightly, I could barely breathe.

"Thank you, Mom," he sobbed into my hair. It was then that I realized how incredibly tall he was. Yes, he'd bypassed me in the height department long ago, but for some reason, now he seemed to stand taller than I'd ever seen him.

Strange.

"Mom, are you okay?" he whispered.

I nodded as I held onto him even more tightly. Meanwhile, Finn helped lower me down to sit in one of the guest chairs in front of the desk, but continued to hover anxiously. He didn't seem to want to let go of me, like he was afraid I'd vanish if he did. I patted Finn's hand where it rested on my shoulder as I tried to reassure him that I was fine. All the while though, I struggled to understand what had just happened to me.

I'd never felt anything like it. Had it been the coven's combined magic that had welled up within me? Had I somehow accessed all of their power through our shared bond? Was that what Wanda felt like all the time? I shook my head and gave a little mental poke at the area where the power had been sitting, and found it still and quiet again, like it had gone back to sleep.

I was definitely going to have to talk to Wanda about this whole magic thing, but at the moment, I had a son to take care of, and a little girl who needed help.

"Easy, sir. Just try to take a few breaths." Andre urged Principal Stillwater to sit back in his chair and laid a gentle hand on his shoulder.

The poor man was sweating and began looking around, appearing entirely baffled. "What in the world is going on?" He frowned as he faced Finn, who was still crying, and then me. Then his attention turned to Andre once more. "Who are you?"

"I'm afraid you've had a bit of a medical emergency, sir," Andre lied smoothly. "Please, just sit tight until help can get here."

Well, it wasn't really a lie. I'd say being turned to gold would classify as a medical issue, especially if the person in question couldn't be turned back. Luckily, whatever the heck I'd just experienced—whatever or wherever that power had come from—it had worked. And I was suddenly so grateful for it—grateful at the same time that it intimidated me.

There wasn't any time to dwell on it, though. So, I shoved the confusion, the exhilaration, and the fear to the back of my mind. We needed to get to Sophie, and we needed to break this Midas curse that was plaguing Mr. Lannister.

I sent a quick S.O.S text to the council group chat, along with the address of the school. With any luck, the cavalry would be here soon. Then I flapped a hand in Andre and Mr. Stillwater's general direction. "Can you stay with him? Make sure he's okay?" I wheezed.

Andre looked torn for a second, as if he wanted to make sure Finn and I were okay, but then he nodded.

I staggered to my feet, with Finn holding me up, and grabbed the handle of my bag. Mr. Stillwater was asking increasingly confused questions, but Andre was doing his best to keep him calm until the others could get there and actually make sure he really was alright.

"Okay." I squeezed Finn's hand. "Take me to Sophie."

Just before the door swung shut behind us, I heard Mr. Stillwater ask in a plaintive voice, "Why am I covered in oil?"

Chapter Fifteen

Finn and I hurried through the halls of the school, and all the while I was so grateful that school was out and, so far, no mundanes had witnessed any of what had happened to Mr. Stillwater.

Finn's shoes squeaked against the tile, the poor guy having to half-drag me along with him as I moved as quickly as my shaking legs would allow me. I still felt hollow and a bit light, like a soap bubble bobbing along on the breeze. And I still couldn't comprehend what had happened in the principal's office, but I was trying not to poke too much at the sleepy, quiet place inside my chest where a storm of magic had just been brewing.

Whatever was going on with me, I needed to

talk to the coven as soon as possible about it.

"Here," Finn panted as we skidded to a stop outside a classroom at the end of the hallway. "This is the science lab."

I could already hear a man's raised voice, even with the door closed. On top of that, there was the sound of muffled sobbing that just tore my heart in half. At the same time though, I was happy to think that muffled sobbing meant Sophie was still Sophie and not a gold version of herself.

I stepped up to the door and glanced through the little window, pressing my head almost flat to the cheap wood to try and see inside. Through the reinforced glass, I could see a girl about Finn's age, huddled into a desk. She was small for her age, dark-haired, her glasses smeared with tears as she clamped both hands over her mouth, trying not to make too much noise as a grown man stood over her, pointing a finger in her face, spittle spraying from his mouth as he yelled.

Oh, heck no.

Forget magic, my inner mama-bear took one look and let out a roar that should have rattled the building to the foundations.

The doorknob rattled in my hand. Locked.

"Finn." My voice came out funny, squeezed out between my clenched teeth. "Open the door for me, buddy."

Finn swallowed, his eyes huge. I rubbed his shoulder as he reached for the door handle, his hand shaking. But with a murmured word, and a light rap on the wood, the knob was instantly turning smoothly under his touch, and the door swung open.

"I want you to wait outside where it's safe," I told him as I turned to face him and gave him an expression that told him not to argue with me.

"Mom, it might not be safe for you," he started, but I shook my head.

"Whatever is going on with my magic... it will protect me." I hoped. I really hoped.

Finn swallowed hard, but then nodded and held the door open for me as he stepped aside and made a point of waiting behind it, where Mr. Lannister couldn't see him.

"If anything goes wrong, you need to run and get Andre," I said.

He nodded again.

Inside, it was easier to both hear Mr. Lannister, and see what was going on. There was a lab bench at the back of the room, with a sink and stools and a sturdy black counter top made to withstand all the punishment the students performing experiments could put it through. Two of the stools had been turned to gold, along with the arched neck of the faucet, but oddly enough, not the rest of the sink. A few golden beakers lay dented on the floor, and my heart clenched with something between terror and rage when I noticed that all of the desks surrounding Sophie had been transformed to glittering metal.

The finger hovering two inches from her sobbing little face wasn't just an expression of fury. It was a threat.

Now, under different circumstances, I might have felt an ounce or two of pity for Mr. Lannister. The Midas curse had certainly taken its toll on him. He looked terrible: gaunt, his eyes sunken back into his skull until he could have passed for an early Halloween decoration. The bones of his face were pressing a little too tightly against his skin, and his hair was greasy, his clothing stained and rumpled, like he'd been wearing it for days and hadn't showered in just as long.

But with the way he was shouting, nearly incoherent, saliva flecking his lips, any pity I might have felt for him faded instantly.

"You did this to me! I know you did, you... you witch! Take it back! *Take it back*!"

He was human, after all. And a science teacher. He'd never had any experience with magic. And now that he'd obviously realized it was real, he was terrified. In his mind, magic had hurt him, deeply—that much was obvious. I could only thank my lucky stars that annoying Kenzie hadn't found him...

As to Lannister, he appeared lost, terrified and furious all at once. But seeing him jab his finger towards little Sophie, and watching her flinch back as she tried to sob silently behind her hands, and I was just suddenly so mad, I could have spit. My vision went red at the edges.

"Get *back*."

Everyone froze. I wasn't someone who raised her voice often. I'd never seen the point. If I couldn't say something calmly, then that meant I should go away and come back to discuss it later when my emotions were under control. Shouting just meant you were out of control, and probably making things worse.

But my command sure surprised Mr. Lannister, who hadn't even realized I was there. It was enough to get him staggering back a few steps on sheer instinct, and that got him out of arm's reach of Sophie. My heart eased a little then, my lungs unlocking so I could take a calmer breath.

While Mr. Lannister blinked at me, his mouth opening and closing slowly, I spoke to Finn out of the corner of my mouth, realizing I'd have to get him involved if I wanted to make sure Sophie escaped.

"I'm going to keep Lannister occupied. Once you can, you get Sophie, and you get out of the room. Do you understand?"

I didn't want to take my eyes off Lannister, but I could tell Finn was nervous—his breath hiccupped a little on the way in. He was scared, and all I wanted to do was to hug him and tell him everything was going to be okay. But I couldn't. I couldn't risk giving Mr. Lannister a chance to pull himself together. Whatever I'd done, whatever my magic had done to free the poor principal from the gold curse, I wasn't sure I had it in me to do it again. Instead of a bonfire, there was nothing but cold ashes in my chest.

I couldn't risk him getting his hands on Finn or Sophie.

"Mom…"

"Finn." It took more control than I was proud of to keep my voice even. "Do you understand?"

He must have heard how serious I was, because he didn't kick up a fuss or insist on playing the hero. He just took a shaky breath. "Yeah, I understand."

"Good."

I took two steps to the side, away from Finn, even though it broke my heart to do it. But I didn't want any of that man's attention on him.

Finn just needed a chance to grab Sophie and get them both out of the classroom. I knew he could do it. I just needed to give him the chance.

Mr. Lannister was focusing on me now, but his eyes were still glassy. Dazed, almost. His forehead was all wrinkled up, like he was thinking hard. Maybe trying to understand why there was a strange adult in his classroom.

My pulse was pounding in my throat, and I wondered if he could see the jump of it. Probably not. I didn't think he was seeing much of anything.

All I wanted to do was get Sophie and Finn and run. But if Lannister came after us, I wasn't sure I could keep him from touching someone and I knew what would follow. And the idea of him touching Finn? I shuddered. It had been bad enough to put my hands on Mr. Stillwater and feel the cool, stiff metal where his skin should have been. I wouldn't have been able to bear it if the same happened to my son.

Just the thought of cold, unfeeling gold creeping over Finn's body, stiffening his limbs, stealing his breath. The thought left my stomach icy with something very close to panic. There was no way in hell I would let that happen. Over my dead body. Or over Lannister's.

I tried to keep the thoughts off my face and

out of my voice. If I was panicked, scared, it might just set him off again. Mr. Lannister had barely looked human when I'd seen him through the door. He was too-thin, too sunken eyed. But up close, well, he looked even worse.

"You're not well, Mr. Lannister," I said, as calmly as I could. "You need help. And I've come here to help you."

He blinked, brow furrowed. "She…" He jabbed a finger towards Sophie, but didn't turn his head away from me. Still, the little girl flinched at the movement. "She did something to me! She… she did something, to my hands. I can't touch things. Everything I touch turns to gold. I can't eat. I can't drink. I… I…"

"I know," I started, but it was like he couldn't even hear me.

"It's her fault." His voice trembled, and I was sure that if he had any moisture left in his body, he would have cried. "It's her fault. I know it is."

Trying to reason with someone who was that sick, and also cursed, probably wasn't going to get me anywhere, but it would keep his attention on me, which was what I wanted. I tried to keep my voice calm, soothing. Like when Finn was a young child and woke up from a nightmare. "Sophie didn't do anything to you, Mr. Lannister."

He glared at me then, eyes wide, his face twisted up in a feral looking snarl. "You're *lying*. She did! It's her fault. She… there was a pencil. And when I picked it up, it was gold, and I couldn't figure out how. But then, once I put it down, anything else I picked up, it turned to gold too! It was her, I know it was!"

My heart lurched with the sudden movement, chills running down my back and legs. The man wasn't just sick, he was edging into something worse. How long could a person go without water? Without food? The man needed help, and he needed it yesterday. Otherwise, I was fairly sure this curse was going to kill him and soon.

From what I'd picked out of his ranting, when Finn had spread his altered potion on the pencil, the super charged *Gypsy Gold* must have soaked into Mr. Lannister's hands when he'd picked the pencil up. And since trying to do something simple, like take a drink or wash his hands or whatever had ended with an entire fountain turning into solid gold, getting the potion off his skin probably hadn't worked out well for him.

I just needed to stall him until Wanda and the others could arrive. She'd be able to remove the curse properly, and then a mundane hospital could do the rest.

"I understand what's happening to you, Mr. Lannister." Keeping my breathing steady was a struggle, but I did my best. Hyperventilating wouldn't exactly help keep me in control. "I can help you. I just need you to calm down, and take a seat."

"No." He shook his head, over and over again, his hands held away from his body like he didn't recognize them. "No, you can't help me. She needs to take it back. She did this to me, it's her fault!"

Even with Sophie out of his line of sight, he was still fixated on her. That wasn't good news. If he realized she was gone, that Finn had managed to sneak her out the door to relative safety, I wasn't sure what he'd do. He couldn't find out. I had to keep his attention on me and me alone.

Sweat beaded at my temples, and I could see the glint of it on my reflection in the gold desk. I slipped a hand into my bag, trying to tell the potions by touch. I knew I'd thrown a bottle of *Fiery Command Oil* in there before I'd torn out of the house. It would only work for a few minutes, but I just needed enough time for help to arrive. And maybe that was the answer.

And if *Fiery Command Oil* had managed to hold off a Wendigo, such as when I'd first moved to Haven Hollow, I was pretty sure it could handle one exhausted, malnourished teacher that looked half dead.

Something moved at the edge of my vision, and my heart clenched so hard in my chest, it felt like it missed a beat.

I should have known. He'd given up way, way too easily.

Finn had gotten Sophie out of the room, just like I'd told him. But then he'd snuck back in, creeping around the edge of the desks, until he was at Mr. Lannister's back. He was pale, and shaking a bit, but his chin was tipped up like he was bracing himself.

And Mr. Lannister was standing between us. He was now between me and my son.

"Sophie didn't do anything to you." Finn swallowed hard enough that I saw the jump of it across the room. "I did."

"No, Finn," I started at the same time that Mr. Lannister froze. It was creepy how still he went, especially after all the frenetic moving he'd been doing. His head turned very, very slowly, until he was facing Finn.

"What?"

His voice was so quiet. A wheeze of air. The only reason I heard him at all was because the rest of the room had gone so painfully quiet, and all my senses were strictly attuned because *that man was between me and my son*.

Finn swallowed again, but he didn't look away or back up. "I did it. But I didn't mean to do it. And I'm sorry. I didn't mean to hurt you. I just wanted you to stop being so awful to Sophie. I never meant for this to happen to you, Mr. Lannister. I'm sorry for what I did, but I know my mom can fix it."

A long, rattling breath came out of Mr. Lannister's throat, and his hands flexed, fingers twisting in the air.

"Finn, back up!" I screamed.

"You…" Mr. Lannister started.

I saw it when his muscles went rigid, when he tensed to lunge at Finn. My heart slammed against my ribs, breath withering away to nothing. My hand jammed to the bottom of my bag. I didn't care what potion I grabbed, it didn't matter, all that mattered was stopping him, getting him away from Finn.

My fingers closed on smooth glass, and I tore the potion out of my bag. I only caught a glimpse of pale lavender glass before I hurled the entire thing at the back of Mr. Lannister's head.

A sleepy time potion that encouraged a good night's sleep probably wasn't the best thing I could have thrown at him, but all it needed to do was just distract him, just get him away from Finn long enough for me to get between them.

I'd already bolted forward when the little glass bottle shattered against the back of Mr. Lannister's head, filling the room with the gentle scent of lavender.

It wasn't heavy glass, and with my numb, noodle arms, I knew I hadn't thrown it very hard. But then, hungry, thirsty, confused, who knew how long it had been since Mr. Lannister had managed to get any rest?

Because the second the sleepy time potion touched him, the moment the oils dripped down his head and neck, the second they soaked into the ragged collar of his shirt, the man's eyes rolled up into his head and he collapsed to the ground, already snoring before he hit the floor.

Finn lunged forward to shove a desk out of the way, to make sure Mr. Lannister didn't hit his head on his way to the floor. With the teacher down, half curled on his side, his hands draped limply together as he breathed deep, we just stared at each other for a second while I tried to coax my heart back down to a rhythm that was more in line for a human than a hummingbird.

Once I caught my breath, I darted forward, and snatched my son into my arms, hugging him tightly, probably tightly enough to hurt, but he didn't complain, he just held me back.

"Don't you ever do that again." Fear made

my voice rough, harsher than I meant it to be. "I'm your mom. It's my job to protect you, not yours to protect me. I mean it, Finn."

"I didn't want him to hurt you," he said in a soft voice.

"It's okay." I stroked his hair back from his forehead, rocking us slightly to the side. And if I used that motion to get Finn a few more feet away from the sleeping Mr. Lannister, well, he didn't seem to notice or if he did, he didn't care.

"Where's Sophie?" I hadn't seen the girl since Finn pulled her out of the classroom.

Finn sniffed, wiping his forearm over his eyes. "I told her to hide in the maintenance closet. That I'd find her when it was safe and I'd explain everything."

"Finn," I said carefully. "You know you can't explain things to her."

He nodded, his eyes still red from crying. "I know. I just… didn't know what else to say. I hate lying to her. But yeah, I know. I really am sorry, Mom."

"I know, buddy."

We were okay. Everything was going to be okay. We could fix it. That was all that mattered.

The door to the classroom screeched open then, dragging against the linoleum, and I shoved Finn behind me, my hand going to my bag, while the quiet, hollow spot in my chest managed a few pitiful sparks in the face of a potential new threat.

But instead of a threat, it was just Wanda.

Her eyebrows slowly climbed up her forehead as she first looked at me and then Finn, then Mr. Lannister, and the amazing gilded mess the classroom had been turned into. Her eyes landed on me once more, where I stood in front of Finn, two random potion bottles held between my knuckles. Her gaze dropped to my chest, and a little wrinkle formed between her eyes.

Slowly, she shook her head back and forth. “I can’t believe you started the party without me.”

Relief made me giddy, a grin stretching my face. “Is Mr. Stillwater, okay?”

“Who?” Wanda rolled her eyes. “Oh, the ex-statue in the front office? He’s fine. Confused as spell, but he’ll live.” She paused to breathe and when she spoke again, her voice was soft. “Are you and Finn okay?”

“We’re fine,” I answered at the same time Finn said, “I’m fine, Aunty Wanda.”

“Aunty Wanda?” I repeated as Wanda gave me a little smile and then waved Finn’s comment away with an unconcerned, manicured hand.

“I might have told your son... at some point... that I wouldn’t have minded if... well, you know.”

“No, actually I don’t.”

She frowned at me. “Leave it to you to make me spit it out.”

“You wouldn’t have minded if what?” I couldn’t help my own smile.

“If I were your sister! There! Are you happy now?” And she even plopped her hands on her hips as she scowled at me.

I walked over to her and threw my arms around her, with Finn quickly following suit. “Well, you’ll always be a sister to me, Wanda.”

“And an aunty to me,” Finn added.

“You both better stop it or you’re going to make my mascara run and then I’ll have no choice but to hex you both.”

Then Wanda turned to face the gold disaster behind us. She gestured to the teacher sprawled on the floor.

“What’s the story with him?”

“He’s our accidental Midas,” I answered on a shrug. “His hands are super-duper cursed, so be careful. I was thinking of dunking them in some *Uncrossing Oil* before he touches anything else? Do you think that would help?”

Wanda pursed her lips as she took a few more steps into the room to peer down at Mr.

Lannister. "It couldn't hurt. Probably."

She glanced at me then, her eyes shifting to Finn. Something like understanding rippled over her face, so of course, she immediately sighed and rolled her eyes like everything in the world was an imposition. "Well, you might as well give the *Uncrossing Oil* to me and go check on Mr. Darcy."

There were times that Wanda did things that reminded me why she was my BFF.

I took Finn's hand, and we headed for the classroom door.

Chapter Sixteen

"Alright, fam," Kenzie Chase whispered into the camera as she slid through the dilapidated door of an old and falling apart farmhouse.

The building's white paint was peeling so badly, it looked like a reptile shedding its skin, and the wood underneath didn't look much better.

"Everyone in this town is really tight-lipped," the menace continued. "They definitely don't like outsiders poking around. But you know Kenzie Chase doesn't give up, and I've finally managed to track down the source of the apparent gold-transformations this town has been seeing."

The door creaked ominously behind her as

she slid it shut, and the feed bobbled a little as she switched from her phone to what looked like a head mounted night-vision camera, if the weird green tinge washing over everything was anything to go by.

The room she walked into looked like maybe once upon a time it had been a kitchen. Time, and the demolition skills of racoons, birds, foliage, rats, and squirrels had left the place a rust streaked, sagging mess. The counter where the sink had once been had caved in entirely. The floors were sagging, and there were paler outlines in the general grime where the refrigerator and stove used to be.

I turned to Henner, who was sitting in the conference chair of Hallowed Homes next to me, happily munching on a bag of kettle corn he'd brought with him. "Where is this place?"

He tossed a kernel and caught it with his mouth, chewing quickly. "It's this old, abandoned place way out at the end of Mill Street. Marty, R.J. and I used to go out there to test our equipment, but there's nothing paranormal there. A few angry raccoons maybe, but it's safe enough structurally."

"Really? It doesn't look very safe," I responded as I frowned and tried to look at the place with a new set of eyes but failed.

"Yeah, we've tugged on the roof and it's not

coming down any time soon," Henner answered.

He chewed another bite, and offered me a handful from the bag, but I turned him down. My stomach was still twisted in knots after everything I'd gone through over the last couple of days. Mr. Lannister's curse had been successfully removed, and all the gold objects scattered around the town had finally been hunted down and returned to their previous condition (courtesy of Wanda and the coven), but no one had ever found any of the missing gold jewelry or antiques, so Taliyah had been pretty annoyed that she still had a bunch of theft reports that weren't likely to be solved any time soon.

Finn was also grounded, and we'd be revisiting the whole 'do not expose mundanes to magic' talk that we'd had as soon as he was old enough to talk. He still felt terrible about the whole situation, so he hadn't protested his punishment at all. I was just glad no one had gotten permanently hurt.

Wanda and the coven had done an excellent job of removing Sophie, Mr. Stillwater, and Mr. Lannister's memories of the event, so at least Finn's friend wasn't flinching at every quick movement or raised voice. And Mr. Lannister had been admitted to the closest hospital to be treated for malnutrition and dehydration, under the guise of a terrible fever that had hit him for a few days. He was responding well, and there weren't any lingering effects expected, which was a huge relief.

But even with all the gold madness resolved and finally put to bed, there was still one, big, annoying loose end to tie up. Just because things had stopped blatantly turning to gold, and none of her videos seemed to make it to her online platforms (courtesy of Henner), Kenzie Chase just seemed more determined to get to the bottom of the 'secret of Haven Hollow', which wasn't ideal for a whole lot of reasons.

The council had come together to debate exactly what should be done about her, but with someone so completely online, who had documented her arrival here, and posted a few clips online before Henner had removed them, just erasing her memory and sending her on her way wasn't likely to work.

So, Henner had proposed something else.

The council had met again at Hallowed Homes, in the big conference room, and Henner had set up his laptop and projected the screen so we could all see the 'show', as he called it.

I still wasn't so convinced about any of it. Kenzie might not have powers, or anything like that, but that didn't mean she wasn't dangerous. The whole ordeal had pointed out to me exactly how thin the veil of safety covering this town really was, and Kenzie's perpetually online presence made me nervous.

I glanced at Henner, who looked totally relaxed in his skeleton hoody, black cargo shorts, black beret and his army boots kicked up onto an empty chair as he snacked. "Are you sure about this?"

"Oh, yeah. Don't worry. The guys were out there before we 'tipped her off'."

"They were out there doing what?" Roy asked.

Henner shrugged. "Oh, you know," chomp, chomp, "just making the place look a bit more run down, and basically setting the stage for a haunting. And, hey, we have to take our fun where we can, right?"

A glance around the table revealed that none of the other council members seemed concerned about what was unfolding before us on the screen and maybe I should have taken my cue from them. Taliyah just looked long suffering. Roy and Fifi were cozied up together like it was a movie date, and Angelo and Wanda looked like they were actively enjoying the showing, making little comments towards the screen.

I let out a breath and tried to shake off the unease. Henner was a good man. Kind, and patient. He had to be, to be dating Darla. My exghost involuntary roommate was nice enough, but she was a lot to deal with 24-7. Henner seemed to enjoy their relationship though, so I was just glad they were happy. The point was, no matter how annoyed he might have gotten with constantly having to thwart Kenzie's more risky videos, Henner would never let her get hurt. Whatever he and his ghost-busting crew had come up with, Kenzie would be safe. And I knew Henner well enough to know that.

My nerves were probably just a holdover from whatever had happened that day in Principal Stillwater's office, when that strange magic had welled up inside me and spilled over. Wanda had taken a look at me later, once everything had calmed down. I'd tried not to get anxious over the baffled expression that had crossed her face before she'd hidden it under a mask of indifference.

"Well, whatever it was, you seem to have worn it out for now, at least," she'd said with a shrug.

The space in my chest had been quiet once I broke the gold curse, but not empty and since then, it had been rebuilding itself. I could feel it.

"So, you think it will come back?" I'd asked Wanda, while twisting the edges of my sleeves repeatedly until she'd grabbed my hands and made me stop.

“Leave your poor clothes out of this, they have enough trouble as it is.” Then she’d sighed. “The power isn’t ‘gone’ now, so it isn’t about it coming back. It’s already there so it can’t come back.”

“So?”

“So, it’s just tired. Spent. When it has some time to recover, we’ll run some more tests.”

“Hmm.”

“It’s fine,” she’d said, waving her hand at me as if it really wasn’t a big deal. “Power is never a bad thing.”

When I hadn’t looked convinced, she’d screwed up her face like she was cleaning up someone else’s vomit, and then patted me on the back. “There, there.”

Wanda’s complete lack of comforting instincts had made me laugh, at least, and some of the worry had faded. Faded, sure, but it was far from gone. I didn’t understand this newfound power and it made me nervous, even if I tried to remind myself that what Wanda had said was true—more power was better than less power. And, really, in this insecure town, I probably needed all the magical mojo I could get.

On the screen, Kenzie took another few steps across the ominously creaking floor. The camera swept left and then right, taking in the room. The light glinted off the broken window where the sink used to be and threw back a glare.

Her voice was low when she spoke, like she was trying to sound spooky. "An old woman told me that a witch used to live in this house. A witch with a spindle made out of gold."

I glanced between Wanda and Henner, frowning. "A witch?"

Henner tossed himself another piece of kettle corn and grinned, chewing. "The last people to actually live there were an insurance salesman and his family, back in the 1950s. But they pulled up stakes and moved when they realized Haven Hollow wasn't the best spot for his business."

"Okay, so where did the witch bit come in?" I asked.

By this point, I was fairly sure Angelo was asleep. At least, his eyes were closed.

Wanda tossed back her head and laughed. "You should've seen Betanya's face when she was feeding this ditz that line about the witch. She looked like she'd bitten into a lemon. It was hilarious."

I couldn't believe they'd actually gotten Betanya to play along, but then, Henner was her only grandchild, so that might have had something to do with it. Or probably all to do with it.

"The witch could use her spindle to weave

things into gold," Kenzie continued. "Things like cloth and thread and chains—really anything she pleased."

"Wait." Fifi blinked, pausing with her hand in the bag of candy corns she and Roy were sharing. "Isn't that the story of Rumpelstiltskin?"

Henner shrugged, unconcerned. "We're ghostbusters, not storytellers."

Kenzie kept moving forward, carefully skirting the edges of the kitchen, away from some of the spots where the floor sagged, and in one spot, I noticed a hole in the rotting boards. And Henner had said this place was safe? I just hoped Kenzie didn't fall through and break her leg, or something worse.

Henner caught my concerned look. "R.J. got a little overly enthusiastic with the sledgehammer, and his foot went through the floor."

"Oh my God," I started, eyes going wide.

"Nah, don't worry about it," Henner answered, shaking his head. "He was just fine. Marty and I pulled him out. Once we stopped laughing, I mean."

Taliyah pinched the bridge of her nose like she had a headache.

The door to the living room was hanging crooked on its hinges, and it took Kenzie a couple tries to get it open. Rusted metal squealed as she finally managed to wrestle the door back. "They say that the witch became obsessed with gold, spinning day and night, and turning everything around her into metal. Even her food. Even her water well. Until she slowly starved to death." Then she paused as she frowned. "Though how you'd spin food into gold or a water well doesn't exactly make sense." But she shrugged and the question was forgotten, at least for now.

"Good question," Roy grumbled as he looked at Henner.

"Hey, I'm just the messenger," Henner shrugged.

I turned back to the camera footage and watched as Kenzie clearly attempted to play things up, to appeal to her audience's ghoulish leanings, but that comment about turning food and water into gold hit a little too close to home. If things had dragged out any longer, if Mr. Lannister hadn't figured out how to get a few sips of water through a golden straw, that very well could have been his fate.

"And some say," Kenzie whispered, the squealing of the door hinges an annoying backdrop. "That her ghost—the ghost of the witch—still lingers here. Still guarding her precious spindle."

She swept the room with her night vision

camera, passing over old, moth-eaten rugs, and a couch that sagged so far in the middle that it was resting on the ground, springs and moth-nibbled foam poking out of it. Over on the far side of the room, by the old, fieldstone fireplace, was a rocking chair that glinted gold in the dark, with a drop spindle resting on the seat.

Kenzie hurried forward, but I frowned, squinting at the lower corner of the screen. "Wait, is that...?"

Henner grinned like a loon, not looking away.

As Kenzie came closer, the dripping lines of gold got more and more obvious. Her foot hit a pile of something that clattered and rolled across the floor, and she stumbled, bending forward to give her viewers a clear shot of the obviously badly painted faux gold cover on the old chair and spindle.

She grabbed one of the things she'd tripped on, holding it up to the light to reveal one of a dozen cans of gold spray paint.

"What the hell? Seriously," she seethed under her breath, and then she threw the empty can into the cold fireplace. There was a click that echoed through the old farmhouse, and something white and billowing dropped from the ceiling, sending Kenzie shrieking and scrabbling backwards. The camera bounced and jostled dizzyingly as she bolted across the room, her heavy breathing filling the air. Finally, she stopped, and spun to press her back to the wall in order to see what had almost fallen on her.

A ghost made out of a bedsheet and some fishing twine, its face of three circles drawn in what looked like black sharpy, dangled from the ceiling, slowly rocking and turning midair where it hung. The guys must have hid it in the rafters, ready to drop when someone messed with the fireplace.

I clasped a hand over my mouth, trying not to laugh. "You didn't."

Henner grinned, unrepentant. "Oh, we did."

"Are you kidding me?" Kenzie whisper-shrieked. "When I find out who did this, I'm going to–"

The rest of her threat was cut off by the sounds of howling coming from directly outside the house. The howls were very quickly followed by a series of bangs on the walls, as though numerous people were drumming their fists against the old wood.

"Oh, my God," Kenzie started, her voice cracking with her pitch. "What the hell is that?"

Soon, the sounds dissolved into laughter and a few more spooky fake ghost sounds that sounded surprisingly like children.

"Louisa Rutlidge's kids were happy to volunteer to perform their civic duty for Haven Hollow," Henner explained, with a straight face somehow.

Wanda cackled. Even Roy let out a snicker.

Kenzie tore through the house then, running for the door in the kitchen she'd just come in through. "Get back here, you little brats!!"

The kids were long gone by the time Kenzie got outside, their fading laughter drowned out by her furious little huffs of breath. Not that she'd ever have a chance of catching a bunch of werewolf kids in the woods.

As a parting gift, the Rutledge kids had thrown some trailing lines of toilet paper over Kenzie's van, which was parked in the old, overgrown gravel driveway. They'd also written 'BOO' on her windshield with what looked like soap, and made a few little ghosts out of tissues to hang in the tree outside, their little plush bodies bobbing merrily.

Kenzie tore her night vision camera off her head and yanked it around so she could speak into it. Her blonde hair was in a wild tangle, and there was a smear of dust or grime down one side of her cheek.

"Okay, screw this town. I'm out of here," she insisted. "Haven Hollow is the worst. I'm sick of my videos not loading, and people giving me garbage stories. I'm out of here."

At that, a little cheer went up in the meeting room.

Kenzie's eyes narrowed, even though there was no way she could have heard us through the camera feed. "But before I get the hell out of here, I'll leave you with this: I know there's something going on in this town. There's a huge cover-up, a conspiracy. No one wants to talk to me about it, but that's fine. Kenzie Chase always catches what she's after."

"Always beware of anyone who refers to herself in the third person," Wanda muttered.

Kenzie's eyes narrowed, and she held the camera inches from her face. "I'll be back to prove it. Just you wait."

It sounded like a threat, and I was pretty sure that was how it was intended to be taken.

The camera feed cut out then, and the council gave a round of applause while Henner pretended to bow, somehow not spilling what was left of his kettle corn. Roy reached over and patted his shoulder with one huge mitt of a hand.

His face falling into more serious lines, Henner rolled up the top of his popcorn bag. "I've corrupted most of her files, even the originals on her phone when she accessed public WIFI. She didn't get anything incriminating on film. It's mostly just her looking dumb."

"Good riddance," Taliyah said, shoving

away from the table.

There was laughter, and general agreement as everyone stood, getting ready to leave. And at that point, Angelo even woke up.

I seemed to be the only one concerned that Kenzie would make good on her threat, and return to Haven Hollow.

I could only hope we'd be ready for her when she did.

Chapter Seventeen

I unlocked my front door and let myself in, giving a big sigh of relief when I finally got to drop my purse on the bench in the front hall.

It had been a long day at the shop, and then with the council meeting afterwards, I was just so glad to be home again. I hung my coat up, kicked off my shoes, and headed for the kitchen to see what I could cobble together for dinner.

My stomach had unknotted enough that I kind of regretted not taking Henner up on his offer of his kettle corn. But with the smell of garlic and butter drifting through the house, I wondered if maybe I wouldn't have to worry about dinner after all. My stomach let out a really embarrassing sound, complaining like I hadn't eaten anything in months.

“Mom?” Finn poked his head out of the kitchen, his arms wrapped around his middle. The smile he shot me was a ghost of its former self, but at least, it was present and accounted for. “There was still some leftover lasagna, so I thought I’d heat some up for dinner.”

“Thank you, Finn. That sounds amazing.” I got onto my tiptoes to brush a kiss over his cheek and went to grab some plates and cutlery for us.

Finn hadn’t quite been himself since the showdown with Mr. Lannister. Now he was just very subdued. I knew he was upset with himself as well as with how everything had turned out. Yes, he’d just been trying to stick up for his friend, and he’d only meant for the *Gypsy Gold* potion to be a little prank, but it had all gotten dangerously out of hand. The council had also called him in and Roy had given him a stern talking to in front of all the other members (who had immediately given him hugs and told him everything was going to be okay). Interestingly, ‘Aunty Wanda’ had been the most protective of Finn and after Roy came close to yelling at him, Wanda had actually stepped in (actually in front of Finn as if she were shielding him) and told Roy to knock it off unless he wanted to be turned into a Redwood.

He’d knocked it off.

But the point was: this entire situation was exactly the reason that magic was kept strictly away from mundanes. Not only was it risking revealing the supernatural to them, but someone could get seriously hurt, or worse.

Still, I hated seeing Finn moping around and blaming himself. That was partially why I'd grounded him in the first place. It was a finite punishment. He could serve his sentence, and then maybe he could forgive himself. But, so far, it didn't seem like that was the case and I wondered if I should have grounded him at all, considering how hard he was being on himself.

We sat quietly while we ate together, making our way through the leftover lasagna and garlic bread and the quick salad I'd whipped up because, as the responsible adult, I felt like it was important for us to have something green on the plate.

Andre had called earlier and asked if he could take us both to dinner, but I'd told him I felt like Finn needed a night with just the two of us. Of course, Andre had been more than understanding and he'd promised to check on us the next day. And I'd felt really good about that—good that I'd put my son first and Andre was not only okay with it, but encouraged it. He was a good man, and I felt beyond lucky to know he was *my* good man.

When Finn was finished eating and just pushing the few last bits of noodle and sauce around his plate, he set his fork down. “Mom, I know I’ve said it a million times before, but I want you to know how sorry I really am,” he said, without lifting his head.

I couldn’t say it was okay, because it wasn’t. But I put my hand on his shoulder and gave it a little squeeze. “I know, honey. I just wish you’d come to me sooner.”

And that was the real problem I was having with the whole thing. While I wasn’t happy with Finn using a potion against his human teacher like he had, I was mostly hurt that, not only hadn’t he brought the problem to me when he’d realized there was one, but he’d lied to me. It was going to take a little while to move past that, especially owing to the fact that Finn hated lies—since it was so easy for him to detect them.

He drooped a bit in his seat. “I should have told you the truth. I was just scared to come to you right away. I thought I could fix it on my own, and... well, I know you don’t like it that I have magic.”

He said the words so nonchalantly that they made my chest hurt. I hadn’t meant to make him feel that way, but I understood why he would. My own fear regarding Finn’s powers had gotten the best of me. I'd been so worried about something happening to him because of his magic, that I'd made my son think I didn't like it that he was gifted.

My chair scraped against the wooden floor as I scooted closer to him. "No, I love your magic. Your gift is beautiful, and I think it's amazing that you can bring hope to so many people. I can't wait to see what your power grows into."

I'd gotten a hint of it this last Christmas, almost a full year ago. I still wasn't sure if what I'd seen was a real vision of the future, or just a projection of my unconscious mind, but the glimpse I'd gotten of my son had been so warm and kind, it still brought a smile to my face. He'd been so secure in his gifts, and I'd never been more proud of anyone in my life. The way he'd moved through the world, making people smile, bringing them hope, it had really been something to see.

I hated the thought that I hadn't shown him how I truly felt. That the way I'd acted, the things I'd said, had made him think I wasn't proud of him, or worse, that I was ashamed of his gifts. Because that couldn't be further from the truth! That realization caught me like a swift hit to the gut.

I gave Finn a one-armed hug, squeezing him

into my side. "I do worry about you. Of course, I worry—I'm your mom. But that doesn't mean I dislike your gift or that I don't like your magic, Finn. I'm always concerned that you might get hurt, or that you might be in danger. And I don't like it that using your power sometimes drains you so terribly, but that doesn't mean I'm not also incredibly proud of you and what you do. And I'm so sorry I made you feel like you couldn't come to me about this. I can understand why you were worried to and I do take some responsibility for that. I want it to be known that I am so happy to know you're a Magician and I support you and your magic fully."

He looked up at me finally, and I smoothed his hair back from his face like I used to when he was a little boy.

"You really mean that?"

I nodded. "I mean it with all my heart, buddy. And, what's more, I want you to know that you can come to me for anything. Anything. No matter what, and I'll help you. If you're ever in trouble, you can tell me. I might be mad or upset, but I'll always help you, Finn. There's nothing I wouldn't do for you and no matter what, I will always love you more than anything in the world."

Finn tilted his head sideways to rest on my shoulder, and he let out a breath. "Thanks,

Mom."

We sat there for a minute, and then I nudged him up. "Why don't you get started on your homework? I'm going to get the dishes cleaned up."

Finn nodded, and while I sorted out the mess left from dinner, he pulled out his books and got to work right there at the old wooden table.

Washing and drying the dishes gave me a few minutes alone with my thoughts. I'd never meant to make Finn think that I didn't approve of his magic. His Magician gift was beautiful, and the things he could do with it were incredible. It had never been about the power, it had been about the kinds of situations his power would drag him into.

But sadly, intent wasn't magical. Not meaning to do something didn't just undo the hurt caused. Wasn't that what I'd told Finn about his prank with the potion? I'd apologized, sure, but there had to be something more I could do. Something that would show Finn that I meant what I'd said, that I supported his magic fully.

I thought about it as I put the last plate away, and then it finally came to me.

Finn was still bent over his math book as I hurried up the stairs to my bedroom. In the closet, up on the shelf, there was a book, the cover made of carefully stitched brown leather, worn and old, and a little cracked in places, but cared for. I lifted it down carefully, enjoying the way the leather warmed under my hand.

My mother had given me that book, a record of every potion she'd ever made. It had been started by her mother, my grandmother, and my great-grandmother before that—the line of my family, who had been Gypsy potion makers since as far back as I could remember, and beyond.

I didn't use it very much anymore. When I'd been a young girl, that book had been my near constant companion. I'd read it over and over again, memorizing every measurement, every instruction, until it had just about become part of me. I still brought it down sometimes, for potions that I didn't make all the time, like I had for *Gypsy Gold*, but mostly the recipe book stayed on its shelf these days, where it wouldn't get torn or damaged.

I brushed my fingers over the leather, remembering long nights and rainy afternoons I'd spent poring over the book. Learning to brew, how to prepare ingredients, how to imbue water and oils and plants and scents, and turn them into magic. Lifting the book close to my face, I inhaled deeply. Leather and lavender, cinnamon, bergamot, jasmine, citrus and other, fainter scents that had soaked into the paper. It brought decades-faded memories swimming to the front of my head.

I carried the book down the stairs and back into the kitchen, where Finn was just packing up his things. He glanced up as I came in, nibbling on his lower lip.

"Is Andre still coming over tomorrow?" he asked, sounding nervous.

"He is. He's coming for dinner."

Finn visibly relaxed, a more genuine smile coming to his face. Not quite his usual sunny grin, but much closer than any of them had been for a while.

While Finn's grounding also meant no magic lessons for a couple weeks, apparently he'd been worried that he wouldn't see Andre at all, or maybe he thought Andre was mad at him. While Andre obviously had been disappointed by the situation, he also understood that Finn's intent hadn't been malicious when he'd made the potion. And Andre was already over it, ready to move on to Finn's next Magician trick.

His gaze dropped to the book in my arms. "What's that?"

He'd seen the book before, of course. Especially when he was younger, and I'd been less confident about my measurements.

"This is my Ouire," I teased, dropping into the chair beside him and placing the heavy book on the table.

"Grandma's recipe book." Finn traced a gentle finger over the lightly cracked leather of the spine. "Are you making a new potion?"

"Not exactly." I opened the book carefully, flipping through the pages until I came to the recipe for *Dreamtime Oil*, smoothing the paper absently with my hand. "This was the first potion your grandmother taught me how to make when I was a little girl. We worked on it together, and she taught me how to brew, how to measure, and how to put my power into the mixture and turn it into a proper magical potion."

All the little notes of generations of Morton women were there—scribbled in the margins: my mother's carefully printed words next to my grandmother's spidery scrawl. There were a few words in Gaelic in the corner that I couldn't read, but that my mother claimed said something about not putting too much cinnamon in the brew, or the dreams it induced might get too spicy.

Holding that book, I felt connected to all the women of my family who'd come before me. It was my tie to my ancestors, but also to our magical heritage. For centuries, we'd been brewing potions to sell and trade, and I was just the most recent to carry on the tradition. I'd always thought I might be the last, entirely.

Magic tended to favor women. It came to them far more frequently and in greater quantity than it ever did to our male counterparts. Oh, sure, there were some exceptions to the rule, like Wanda's cousin, Maverick. But for the most part, you'd get a hundred witches for every warlock. No one quite knew why for sure.

So, when I'd had a son instead of a daughter, I'd assumed I'd be the last potion brewer in the family. Finn had always had his gifts, the men in my family tended to. But being able to hear a lie, or sniff out a mushroom wasn't the same as making a potion or casting a spell, not really. Finn turning out to be a Magician, and a strong one at that, had sure been a surprise.

The fact that he'd managed to make the *Gypsy Gold* potion at all was pretty impressive. Okay, sure, it hadn't exactly come out the way he'd intended it to, but it had still worked. And, in fact, his version had been much stronger than the original. The point was: his magic had gone into the mixture and it had created a potion that worked. It made me wonder if I'd been a bit too premature in putting Mom's book away.

Finn was smiling, reading over my grandmother's notes on moon phases, and how the *Dreamtime Oil* needed to rest in the light of a full moon, his lips moving silently as he read the words on the page. I couldn't help but smile at the way his brow furrowed in concentration, like he thought there was going to be a test or something.

When he finally looked away from the page, I smiled at him.

"So, what do you think?"

Finn's brows pinched together in puzzlement. "Think? I mean, it's really cool. I like all the little notes. It's like a bunch of people all giving advice at the same time."

He wasn't wrong. It was especially true of the parts where, some great, great aunts of mine had gotten into an argument right in the margins, each scribbling out the other's notes until they'd finally declared a truce.

"It is cool. But what I meant was: what do you think about you brewing a potion with me?"

The way Finn's whole face lit up was like watching the dawn break through the clouds, and it made something warm and golden kindle in my chest.

"Really? Like you'll teach me how to make potions?"

I nodded. "Sure. If you want to?"

"Yeah, I definitely want to!" He was almost bouncing in his seat with excitement.

I couldn't hold that golden light in any

longer, and it bubbled up and out of my throat in a delighted laugh. "Why don't you pick out the sprig of lavender we use? Make sure it isn't too crumbly."

Finn leapt up to run to the cupboard where I kept my potion ingredients, moving across the floor like he had wings on his feet.

I watched him go with a soft smile, and something warm and content in my heart.

~~~~

The End

Return to Haven Hollow in:

Newlywed and Pixie-Led

Haven Hollow #28

(*Princess Procedural*)

by J.R. Rain & H.P. Mallory!

Available now!

If you enjoyed Gypsy *Gold*, please help spread the word by leaving a review.

Thank you!
~~~~

GYPSY GOLD

About J.R. Rain

J.R. Rain is the international bestselling author of over seventy novels, including his popular Samantha Moon and Jim Knighthorse series. His books are published in five languages in twelve countries, and he has sold more than 3 million copies worldwide.

Please find him at: www.jrrain.com.

About H.P. Mallory

H.P. Mallory is a New York Times and USA Today bestselling author. She has eleven series currently and she writes paranormal fiction, heavy on the romance! H.P. lives in Southern California with her son and a cranky cat.

To learn more about H.P. and to download free books, visit: www.hpmallory.com